HE ER

BROKEN HEARTS ACADEMY BOOK 2

C.R. JANE

Heartbreak Lover by C. R. Jane

Copyright © 2020 by C. R. Jane

All rights reserved.

No portion of this book may be reproduced in any form or by any electronic or mechanical means, including information storage and retrieval systems, without written permission from the author, except for the use of brief quotations in a book review, and except as permitted by U.S. copyright law.

For permissions contact:

crjaneauthor@gmail.com

This book is a work of fiction. Names, characters, businesses, places, events, locales, and incidents are either the products of the author's imagination or used in a fictitious manner. Any resemblance to actual persons, living or dead, or actual events is purely coincidental.

Cover: Eve Graphic Design

Editing: Heather Long

Proof: Bookish Dreams Editing

For you. You know who you are.

JOIN C.R. JANE'S READERS' GROUP

Stay up to date with C.R. Jane by joining her Facebook readers' group, C.R.'s Fated Realm. Ask questions, get first looks at new books/series, and have fun with other book lovers!

Join C.R.'s Fated Realm

HEARTBREAK LOVER

"I'll ruin us," Jackson whispered to me in the dark.

No one wants to believe in monsters, but I've seen firsthand that they exist.

I'd said goodbye to Jackson Parker, desperate to save myself once and for all, but old habits die hard.

When a monster from the past comes back, I will have no choice but to reveal our secrets.

I need Jackson to be my hero, but he has his own scars.

Can we conquer the past once and for all? Heartbreak Prince or lover...there's a fine line that separates the two.

I once said I would love him forever, but at what price does forever cost?

Dear lord, when I get to heaven
Please let me bring my man
When he comes tell me that you'll let him in
Father tell me if you can

-Lana del Rey

HEARTBREAK LOVER SOUNDTRACK

you broke me first
(Tate McRae)

July
(Noah Cyrus)

Sparks
(Coldplay)

All Too Well
(Ruston Kelly)

Impossible
(James Arthur)

Jar of Hearts
(Christina Perri)

Clean
(Taylor Swift)

Heartbreak Lover Soundtrack

Scumbag
(Goody Grace)

Hold On
(Chord Overstreet)

Young And Beautiful
(Lana Del Rey)

Heart Beat Here
(Dashboard Confessional)

Wild Horses
(The Rolling Stones)

Sad Beautiful Tragic
(Taylor Swift)

Iris
(The Goo Goo Dolls)

Two
(Sleeping at Last)

Wildflower
(5 Seconds of Summer)

Listen to the full soundtrack here.

JACKSON

Have you ever sat in the dark and made friends with your sins?
I do it all the time.
There's only one real sin that I need atonement for though.
And I gave up trying to gain my penitence for her a long time ago.

EVERLY

I still miss you.

You probably wouldn't believe that after everything that has happened between us. But when I close my eyes, it's only your blue gaze that I see.

It's only your hands that I imagine tracing my skin. It's only your body that I crave when I wake up in the middle of the night, tangled in my sheets, as my body tries to torture me with memories of what you felt like moving inside of me.

I miss your voice. I miss your laugh.

I even miss your anger.

Am I sick? You would say no, but only someone that was broken could ever want the person who did the breaking as much as I want you.

My mother's been an addict her whole life. Whether it was my father, popularity, money, or alcohol.

And I used to think she was weak.

But then I got a taste of you, and now I think I understand her a little bit more than before.

I look for you in crowds. Your name is the only prayer on my lips. The only altar I worship on is yours.

I'm sick. But you made me this way.

But even knowing that you're inside of me, wreaking havoc with my vital organs, I still can't get enough.

I still miss you.

But I'll never tell you that.

1
THEN

Jackson

I knew she was gone before I even opened my eyes. The loss of her presence was tangible in the room. It was like she'd taken something with her and now my bedroom felt lacking, despite the magic that we'd created together just a few hours ago.

It wasn't just her absence that had me feeling off, there was a foreboding sensation settling onto my skin. And it wasn't going away.

Grabbing my phone, I looked to see if she had sent me a text explaining why she'd fled. A flash of lightning lit up my room just then.

She'd fled in a storm no less.

My heart started skipping in my chest when I saw that I had ten missed calls.

None were from her though. Instead, they were from my father.

Odd that they just didn't come knocking on the pool house door if whatever they needed was so pressing.

Getting out of bed, I slipped on a pair of basketball shorts as I called my dad back.

"I've been trying to call you for a fucking hour. What have you been doing?" my dad barked.

"I've been asleep. It's two in the morning," I responded snottily as anxiety punched me in the gut.

My dad broke down just then. My whole life, the man had been a pillar of stoicism, hardly ever showing emotion. But he was sobbing into the phone like he'd just found out he was terminal or something.

"Dad—"

"It's Caiden. He was in an accident. He's in the hospital."

His voice cut off as his sobs worsened. My heart clenched in my chest. I ran to my dresser and was throwing a shirt on before my dad continued.

"We're at Southridge Presbyterian. Just get here quick," he finally said before hanging up the phone.

Once inside my truck, I tried to dial Everly. Maybe she had gotten freaked out that she'd given me her virginity and needed to get away?

I shook my head as soon as I had that thought. What we'd shared tonight was fucking magic. The stuff that sonnets and songs were written about. I wasn't going to let her regret me...regret us. We would figure everything out.

Everly's phone went to voicemail.

"Everly," I began, my voice breaking. "I'm not sure where you went, but something has happened to Caiden and I'm headed to the hospital right now. If you could come whenever you get this message... It's really bad." I took a deep breath. "And just in case we don't get to talk about it right away, tonight was the best night of my life and I'll never regret it. I love you more than life itself. Call me."

I blew out a sigh, my gut clenched with worry, and I drove like a maniac towards the hospital. A storm was raging, and the roads were slick. I had trouble seeing through the sheets of rain, but somehow, I made it without crashing.

I parked and ran through the rain to the hospital entrance.

"Caiden Parker?" I barked at the front desk.

The tired looking woman seemed unimpressed with the urgency in my voice. "Are you a family member?"

"I'm his fucking brother," I hissed, exhausted myself. I glanced around towards the waiting room, half expecting Everly to be there waiting. But she was nowhere to be seen.

"Identification?" she asked, and I pulled out my duct tape wallet that Everly and I made together and handed her the ID.

She finally handed it back to me after typing on her keyboard for what felt like fifteen hours. "He's in room three-oh-five. The elevators are to your left."

"Thanks," I answered insincerely before racing to the elevator. I took a quick look into the mirrored walls to check the color of my eyes. I breathed an inward sigh of relief when they looked as blue as ever. I couldn't really tell when I was going to get speedy. I didn't recognize that I was acting different. But my eyes could usually tell me. Now was not the time for me to descend into one of my cycles.

The elevator doors finally opened, and I felt like I'd been to war and back by the time I got to Caiden's room. I came to a screeching halt when I saw Caiden, lying there on the hospital bed, his body covered in blood, bruises, and bandages.

Phantom pain crawled all over my body, as if the twin

connection was real and I experienced a portion of what he had to be feeling.

He was lying there, as still as a statue, and my heart felt like someone had reached inside my chest and grabbed it in a stranglehold.

My parents were holding each other in an armchair by the bed. When my mother looked up from my dad's shoulder and saw me, she burst into fresh tears and jumped up from the chair. She rushed at me, throwing herself in my arms, her sobs filling up the whole room.

"Mom, tell me he's okay," I choked out. I didn't know what I would do if something was majorly wrong with him. Caiden was my twin, half of my soul. I couldn't imagine a world where he wasn't by my side.

I pushed away the feeling of guilt that was battering at my skin over Everly. Caiden would understand when I told him how I felt. He would understand that I needed Everly to breathe. It had never been like that for him.

He would understand.

"He's just sleeping, son," my father said, walking over to where I was trying to comfort my mother and clapping me on the shoulder. For a second, it almost looked like he was going to hug me. I would have known things were really bad then. Since the moment that I'd received my bipolar diagnosis, I hadn't received another hug from my father.

I had come to peace with that.

I breathed out a sigh of relief that my mother's hysterics didn't seem to match the situation.

Just asleep. I could work with that. Whatever Caiden needed, I would be there for him. Physical therapy, driving him around, bringing him food...whatever he needed.

Except her, a voice laden with guilt whispered in my head.

My father extricated my still sobbing mother off of me, and I pulled out my phone, frowning when I saw that Everly hadn't responded back to me yet.

This wasn't like her. Sighing, I sent her another text before returning my phone to my pocket and turning my attention back to Caiden and my parents.

"What's wrong with him? What happened? Why was he driving in the storm?" I asked, the questions falling out of me quicker than they could answer.

My mother's sobs abruptly stopped, and anger crashed over her features. She opened her mouth to say something, and then we heard a low groan.

Caiden was waking up.

My mother and father hovered around his bed, gazing at him hopefully. I took a step forward to join them but then stopped, something making me hesitate. I gazed at the picture the three of them made, the adoring parents with their golden son. It was a little ironic that I was the one that had inherited the golden looks. It had been the three of them since my issues had started, with me standing on the outside looking in.

I shook off the sick feeling I had and forced myself to walk to Caiden's bedside.

He groaned again. His eyes slowly blinked open, and my mother started crying again, this time hopefully tears of relief.

His gaze flicked over to mine, confused, and I let out the breath I'd been holding since I'd heard the news. He was awake. Everything was going to be all right if he was awake.

Something flickered in Caiden's gaze as he stared at me, something I'd never seen there before...something that looked a lot like hate.

But he couldn't know what I'd done last night. There

was no way. And he would understand once he did know. He would want me to be happy. He would want her to be happy.

I just knew it.

"Caiden," I breathed, brushing my hair out of my face with a shaky hand.

He was giving me that look, and then it was like a jolt of lightning struck him. He sat straight up, groaning as he did so, a look of panic plastered across his face.

"Everly!" he screamed frantically. "Where is she?" He looked all over the room as if we were hiding her in a closet. "Everly!" he screamed again.

My parents had jumped up and were trying to get him to lay back down, but I was frozen in place, trying to understand why he was calling her name like that.

"Caiden, I'm sure she will be here soon. I left her a few messages. She's probably just sleeping."

"Everly!" he screamed again as he suddenly punched my dad full in the face, knocking him down to the ground as he struggled to unhook the wires and tubes.

I finally came to my senses and grabbed him, holding him down to the bed as my mother rushed out of the room to call the nurses for help.

"She'll be here soon, bro. You need to calm down," I reassured him through clenched teeth as he landed a hit to my left ribs.

"She was in the car," he cried out, panicked. "She was in the car." I'd never heard him sound like that.

It took me a full minute to grasp what he was saying, and when I did, my blood ran cold. And now it was me panicking.

"Everly was in the car?" I gasped. "What do you mean?

Where is she? Is she okay?" The questions rushed out of me just like when I'd been asking my parents about him.

I felt sick to my stomach when he shook his head and a tear rushed down his face. "She was in the car, Jackson. Please just find out how she is," he begged me.

"Stay in this bed," I snarled out to him before letting go of him and rushing out of the room. My mother was screeching at the nurses in the hallway, telling them they needed to get "their asses" into the room and help her son.

I ignored her and ran over to the desk where a nurse was sitting, rolling her eyes at my mother's antics.

I didn't blame her.

But I was going to be making an even bigger scene if someone didn't tell me where Everly was…and fast.

"Everly James," I told her, tapping my fingers nervously on the edge of the counter. "Is she at this hospital? What room is she in?" Tears got caught in my throat, and for a second, I was a little ashamed that I didn't have any tears for the guy I shared a womb with, but one mention of Everly possibly being hurt and I was a goner.

"Slow down, son," she said soothingly as she began to type on her computer. "Is she the girl who came in with Mr. Parker?"

"I think so," I told her quickly, although now that I was thinking about it, I couldn't understand why Everly would have been in the car with Caiden. Why would she leave my bed to go be with him? It didn't make any sense.

"Hmmm," she muttered, jarring me from spiraling thoughts.

"What?" I asked desperately.

"It says here she's in surgery. Critical condition in fact."

"Critical condition." I repeated the words slowly, not understanding them.

The nurse nodded sympathetically, obviously seeing the devastation written all over my face. "I'll let you know as soon as I hear anything. But she doesn't look good, sweetheart," she said softly.

I suppose I should've backed off and just gone and waited, grateful for the information that she'd given me when she didn't have to give me anything. But I couldn't. "Please, tell me what her injuries are," I begged. A cry slipped from my lips. It felt like I was dying. I needed to be with her. She shouldn't be alone. "Please, she's everything to me."

The nurse looked conflicted, HIPAA rules and all that weighing on her mind, I was sure. But I didn't think it was often you saw a guy my size, weeping like a child. She looked around her, I assumed to make sure that no one was listening, and leaned in.

"I can only go by what's on her chart, but at least preliminarily, she's been diagnosed with a broken femur, a broken arm, a ruptured spleen, punctured lungs, and a traumatic brain injury...and severe lacerations to her face. She arrived at the hospital unconscious. I'm so sorry, honey."

I swayed on my feet, the air in my lungs feeling like it had disappeared. "Is she going to live?" I asked hoarsely. The edges of my vision were starting to shrink in. I was either having a panic attack or an episode, neither of which I could afford at the moment.

Little angel. The words flowed from my thoughts to my lips until I repeated them over and over again nonsensically.

"Someone get a hospital bed. He's about to crash," the nurse yelled as she peeled herself out of her seat.

The next thing I knew the world had disappeared.

Little angel.

I woke up to my parents' heated voices nearby.

"It's all that slut's fault," my mother was raging.

"Does she have a cunt made of gold?" my father retorted.

It took me a second to get it, and then I was the one raging when I realized who they must be talking about.

"Don't fucking talk about her like that," I spat. My parents abruptly stopped talking, and then my mother appeared at the foot of my bed, wringing her hands.

"You're awake," she remarked calmly, because evidently, it was only time for hysterics when her perfect child was unwell.

"Any updates on Everly?" I asked as I heaved my legs to the side of the bed in a mimicry of Caiden's previous movements. Unlike with Caiden, both my parents just kind of watched as I disconnected the IV and got out of bed.

"Don't you want to know what happened?" came my brother's rough voice. I belatedly realized they'd set me up on a hospital bed right next to him.

"What I want to know is how she is. The nurse..." My voice caught. "Her injuries weren't good. The nurse didn't know if she would make it."

Caiden closed his eyes, and tears started to stream down his face. He clenched his lips together, and I could see a pulse in his cheek. "Fuck."

"Everly is in surgery still, boys," my father tried to say calmly, even though I could see that it took a ridiculous amount of effort. My parents had always hated Everly because of her parents. Evidently, Dad had a business partner who had lost a little bit of money to Everly's dad, and my father couldn't ever get over it. Nothing was more important than the money in his and his friend's bank account, after all.

"Can you guys go get me something to eat?" Caiden asked pathetically. I rolled my eyes as my parents nodded and rushed out of the room, obviously not seeing his request for what it was...a desire to talk to me alone.

My gut clenched in desperate worry for Everly. I didn't have time to listen to Caiden. I needed to find out where Everly was in surgery. I could just hover in the halls, send moral encouragement, prayers, good thoughts. I would do anything.

"I know she fucked you," Caiden announced suddenly, and I was immediately paying attention. He was staring at the wall in front of him, not sparing me one glance, even though he had to have known that his words were literally bullets to my chest.

"W-what?" I stammered, not prepared for this conversation. "Look I can explain..."

"She played both of us. We've been having sex all summer. She just decided that I wasn't enough." Emotion crashed through his words. "She called me right after you fell asleep, wanting to meet up. We had sex in the car, and then she told me that she'd fucked you. She was fucking bragging about it. And that's why I crashed."

He clenched at his hospital sheet fiercely before his dark gaze finally connected with mine. "I love her," he told me brokenly. "I love her so fucking much. I don't know how she could have done this."

There was a darkness spreading through my blood. It was thick and poisonous, moving through my arteries and then my veins, pumped through my body by my dying heart.

There was a faint buzzing in my ears.

Caiden was still talking, but I couldn't hear anything that he was saying. It was like my body had shut down with the news that I'd been betrayed by the girl that I'd pledged my fucking soul to. My skin felt itchy and tight, like you could touch me and it would shatter into a million pieces. What went wrong? How did the girl that I'd fallen in love with as a child become a monster? How did we get to this point, where the person I thought I'd known better than anyone could turn around and stab me in the back? *I guess the apple didn't fall far from the tree*, I thought bitterly, thinking of how Everly James could have given her father a run for his money.

I'd never been able to tell without looking at my eyes when the blackness was descending, but here in this moment, I could feel it. And I welcomed it. Because it meant that I wouldn't have to think, that I wouldn't have to feel.

"Jackson," my brother said sharply, my hearing suddenly returning. But I just smiled crazily, glad that soon this nightmare would be over.

Caiden kept calling my name, but I didn't answer. I didn't even know if I was breathing anymore.

And I welcomed the blackness that I'd always detested with every fiber of my being. In that moment, it was my most prized possession.

⁂

CAIDEN BRIBED a nurse for some fentanyl while I was gone to the void inside of me. I didn't know if he was trying to kill himself, or if he just wanted some fucking relief.

As a family, we never really acknowledged what he did. It was always her fault. The bitch that had wrapped herself around both Caiden's heart and mine, and then squeezed until they both burst open and bled out.

So no, I didn't know why my brother took that drug.

All I knew is that he didn't wake up.

He didn't wake up...until now.

Only News. Never Opinions.   **12 Nov**

Dayton Valley News

Your Best Source of News Since 1965

Miracle Recovery After Two Years Asleep

Two years ago the Dayton community suffered an enormous loss when Caiden Jackson, the local football hero, sustained injuries in a car accident. He has spent the last two years in a coma with little hope of recovery. It was announced today that Parker has woken up from the coma. Doctors are calling it a miracle. Caiden is said to be weak, but in otherwise good health, and doctors are positive about his prognosis. Caiden's parents provided us with the following exclusive statement: "Our family's prayers have been answered and we are so grateful for the staff at Memorial Hospital for the excellent care they have provided. We can't wait to see what Caiden -
Story Cont. A3

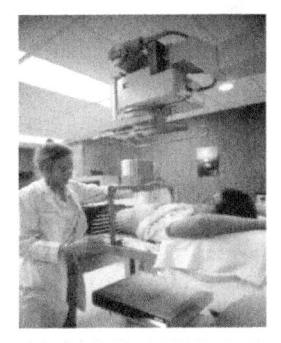

2

NOW

Jackson

It was a bit surreal to see my brother sitting up and laughing with my parents, who suddenly looked like they were ten years younger.

I'd haunted this room for the past few years, prayed to its walls and wished that it was me. And now...it was almost like it had never happened. Sure, Caiden was a ghost of himself, his limbs shrunken with disuse, and I'm sure I would find out soon what else was wrong with his body... But his laugh, my parents' smiles? They took me back.

To a time when I could smile too.

"Jackson!" Caiden cried when I finally knocked on the doorway hesitantly, once again feeling awkward about ruining their picturesque family tableau.

"Caid," I quietly responded in a choked-up voice as I hurried to his bedside and sat down in a chair beside it. My parents looked almost annoyed to see me, even though they'd been the ones to call. I avoided looking at them anymore and just paid attention to the miracle I had in front of me.

"How do you feel?" I asked, trying to hold back the traitorous liquid that was threatening to fall. I'd promised myself I wouldn't cry anymore. I'd done my fair share of crying for my brother...and for Everly.

And I'd vowed to myself it would stop.

I guessed I'd lied to myself just as much as everyone else around me.

Caiden brushed a hand through his hair that was badly in need of a trim. The staff had given him regular haircuts, but there must have been something about being comatose that just gave you a sort of homeless look.

"I mean, I just found out I've lost two years of my life. How would you feel?" he answered, but surprisingly, the words didn't come out bitter. My brother was way better than me. I was bitter down to my core, and I wasn't the one who'd been in a coma.

"Dad...Mom...can you guys go ask if I can have something to eat?" He held up the feeding tube that had been keeping him alive these past years. "I'd love to get something a bit more solid."

My parents immediately agreed and rushed out of the room. Something in my stomach clenched at the easy way he'd manipulated them.

It reminded me of that night. The night that I did my best not to think about anymore.

Especially because...

Fuck. How fucked up was I that I missed her, even as I sat next to my brother, the boy she'd ruined?

Really fucked up.

I was missing *her* right now.

My brother waited for them to leave and then for their footsteps to fade away before he leaned close to me.

"They won't talk to me about Everly. Have you seen her? Is she okay? All I know is that they'd told me I'd been in some kind of car accident and she was with me. I'm freaking desperate to see her. Can you call her? And get Mom and Dad to give me a break? They're driving me crazy."

I stared at him for a second, his words not making sense. Did he mean what I thought he meant?

"You don't remember the accident?" I clarified carefully.

His breath rushed out in a *whoosh*. "I can't remember anything, bro. Maybe our birthday party? I think I remember that. All my memories are scrambled, disjointed."

My mouth opened and then closed again. I had no idea what to say. Was this normal? Would his memories come back?

Did I even want his memories to come back?

I thought the answer was fucking no. An evil thought formed in my brain, grasping onto all my brain cells and infecting me until there was no other path forward than the one I'd just thought of.

The one that was so wrong.

If I could prevent my parents from saying anything...and I never said anything...

Caiden, Everly, and I were the only ones that really knew what had happened that night.

A path had opened up to make Everly mine without all the consequences there had been before.

Even if she was the worst kind of devil, my body craved her and would gladly go to hell with her if it meant we were together. My lines had become blurred over the past few months, good and bad intermixing until I couldn't tell which was which.

I no longer cared that Everly had a soul as black as death.

I only know that without Everly James, I was a dead man walking. She was the only one that could save me.

"Jackson?" Caiden pressed.

"Everly's fine. Things are just a little different now. We had a little falling out after your accident, but everything's good again," I lied.

Everything would be good again, as soon as I was able to see her.

"Everything's good?" Caiden asked. There was a tic dancing by his left eye, and I stared at it absentmindedly as I thought about how I was going to make things right with Everly. Maybe the tic was a byproduct of the coma.

"Or at least it will be good," I admitted grudgingly, taking a step back as I thought about that night.

"Goodbye Jackson," she'd whispered, shattering my soul in that way that only she knew how to.

She'd meant that goodbye, even if all her other words to me had been nothing but lies.

It would take some work to get her back.

"Well, can you call her? Tell her I'm awake?" my brother pushed.

My attention snapped back to him, and this time, I really looked at him. I saw his sunken eyes, his gaunt cheekbones, the waxy pallor of his skin. My brother's body had been a shining example of what the male specimen was capable of achieving before the coma. Now he looked like he'd been on the streets starving for years, everything about him withered and worn.

I would make it right with Everly. But I needed to make it right with my brother before that.

Surely helping him recover would make up for stealing a girl he'd called the love of his life.

Or at least, that was another of the lies I told myself.

Because one thing was for sure. I loved my brother more than I loved myself.

But I loved Everly James even more.

3

Everly

Heartbreak was a sickness. It took over your entire body, and if you were lucky enough to recover from it, you were no longer the same person that you were before.

Just like my body wasn't recognizable after my crash that night with his brother, the ending of whatever had been between Jackson and I transformed my soul into something I no longer recognized.

I was a stranger in my own body. And it was all my fault.

It's been three months since I last really saw him.

I saw glimpses of him—the back of his head, the side profile of his face. I'd hear the sound of his voice...but then he was gone again, and I was left in this strange vortex where I was in love with a ghost.

I'd tried to rebuild my life.

But it was hard when he'd shown me colors I couldn't see with anyone else.

It would have been hard enough just to lose Jackson.

But the news that Caiden had woken up? That was the nail in the coffin.

Every day was a waiting game. I looked for two people everywhere I went nowadays, Jackson...and Caiden.

Caiden waking up should have been freeing, the weight of my guilt lessened by his miraculous recovery.

I hadn't anticipated the nightmares it would bring to have him once again walking among the living. I thought I'd come to peace with the horror of that night, that I'd successfully pushed it away into a little box that I no longer thought about.

But hearing that he woke up brought it all back.

"You made me do this. This is your fault. You knew I wouldn't let you break up with me. You knew it."

The venom in his voice, the strength in his fist, the madness of the moment...it echoed around me on repeat.

It felt a little bit like I was going mad.

"Hey, sweetheart." Landry smiled as he sidled up next to me and put his arm around my waist.

That was another thing that had changed since I'd finally broken it off with Jackson. Landry and I were dating.

If you asked Landry, he would probably tell you that we were getting serious.

I wasn't sure what I would say if asked that question.

As a boyfriend, Landry was the stuff dreams were made of. He was kind and patient, always wanted to see me, complimented me constantly, was gorgeous, and he could make me laugh.

I should have been over the moon to be dating someone like him.

He went out of his way to make me happy.

I should have been happy.

But the sickness Jackson had given me, the heartbreak

that wouldn't let me go...it was an infection that didn't go away.

As he brushed a kiss against my face, I tried not to cringe. "How was class?"

I plastered a smile on my face and looked up at him. He was beautiful, there was no getting around it. His emerald eyes combined with that russet colored hair and a killer smile were hard to beat. I should have been proud to walk on his arm around campus.

I noticed Lane frowning as she looked at me. She'd just recently put bright pink streaks in her hair as part of a "self-enlightenment" stage she claimed to be going through, and I was digging it. Not everyone could pull off walking around with rainbow colored hair on a campus as conservative and uptight as this one, but she rocked it. Lane also rocked at seeing right through me.

I hadn't told her the details of what happened that last night in the library with Jackson. And she didn't know that the fact that Caiden Parker had woken up was making me wake up in a cold sweat every night.

She would comment on the circles under my eyes, but I would blame them on Melanie, who was in fact contributing to my lack of sleep.

Melanie was a demon, to be blunt. The kind that made you sleep with one eye open. I'd gone to administration to request a room change, but they'd told me that there were none available. What they should have said was that there were none available for a scholarship student because, that would have been far closer to the truth.

Things frequently disappeared from my room. I'd had to start storing things in Lane's room, which I hated to do since she was low on space to begin with, but it was necessary. Melanie had "accidently" poured soda all over me the other day while I was sitting doing my homework, and she'd stolen my clothes from inside my shower stall. She always denied that all the little things that happened were because of her, but come on, I'd literally watched her paint her nails the same color blue as the hand that had reached into the stall right in front of me.

Melanie's actions seemed to be escalating, and I didn't know why. I'd come to no rational answer for why she did the things that she did. I still hadn't found out who had performed all those nasty tricks on me those first couple of months, but now that Jackson and I weren't speaking and hadn't seen each other, nothing major had happened.

I tried to convince myself it couldn't possibly have been Jackson. I really did.

Needless to say, most of my life was not going well.

"Does that sound good, babe?" Landry asked as he stroked the skin in between my jeans and my shirt that had pulled up while I was walking. I counted to three in my head before shifting so he had to move his arm, hoping that the extra time made it less obvious I just didn't want him to touch me.

"Does what sound good?" I asked, blushing as Lane and Landry both frowned at the fact that I hadn't been paying attention.

"The hockey team's having a party after the championship game whether we win or lose. I told you about this," Landry answered, frustration leaking into his voice.

I studied him, admiring the way his shirt fit tightly across his broad shoulders and chest. I tried to will myself to feel more, to be healthy mentally for once in my life.

It was a losing battle.

"That sounds great," I told him, even though the prospect of going to a school party gave me hives. Things may have been quiet, but I was still wary of any school functions. They hadn't exactly been good experiences for me.

Landry checked his watch. "Shit, five minutes to the bell and my class is across campus." He grabbed my face suddenly, leveling me with a passionate kiss that should have knocked my socks off or had me dragging him to the nearest supply closet.

Instead, I felt nothing.

"Bye," I told him half-heartedly, wondering how long I could keep this up.

"See you after class, sweetheart." He strode off to class, garnering stares from both guys and girls alike as he went.

"What is wrong with you, woman?" Lane hissed as soon as he was out of earshot.

"I don't know what you're talking about."

"I'm talking about the fact that you have that boy absolutely tied up in knots, and I get the feeling you couldn't care less."

I sighed as we began to walk to the building that housed my next class with Professor Brady, a class that Jackson had evidently transferred out of, since I hadn't seen him. "Is it that obvious?"

"Evidently not, since he's gone for you. But hell, you could at least smile at the guy. You could do far worse."

What if the guy who was far worse was what I craved with every cell of my being? What was I supposed to do then?

Lane grabbed my shoulder and stopped me. "Look, I know you've held out on me with what happened with Jackson—"

I opened my mouth to deny, deny, deny, but she wasn't having it.

She shook her head. "I'm not an idiot. There were literal

sparks shooting between the two of you, even if you were across the green from each other. You were insane there for a couple of months...and then all of a sudden, he's a ghost on campus and you start to act totally different." She sniffed. "I understand why you didn't tell me at first, but your refusal to still talk about it is a little hurtful."

I was sick with shame. Lane had been nothing but a loyal, ride-or-die friend since I'd met her, even when the easier path would have been to shun me like Melanie and her cohorts.

The bell sounded from the building in front of us. Hopefully, Professor Brady would take it easy on me since this would be my first tardy. The professors here were a little nuts about timeliness...as Lane had warned me that first day.

I brushed hair out of my face as I turned to face Lane. "Everyone that I've ever cared about in my life has let me down, Lane. And not just let me down, but demolished me into a million pieces along the way. I don't know how to trust anymore. I think it's been erased from my DNA."

Lane's lower lip trembled in something that unfortunately looked a lot like pity. But then she surprised me by hooking her arm with mine and dragging me off to my building. "Oh, lady, we'll work on your trust issues, and soon enough, you'll be telling me just how big Jackson's dick really is."

A laugh barked out of me, and she hooted. "I knew it! You have slept with him."

I didn't confirm or deny, and she stomped her foot. "I'll get it out of you one way or another. My dad once wrote a book all about certain torture methods they use in the CIA, so I know things."

She was like a little chihuahua, and I threw back my

head and laughed, garnering an unimpressed look from Professor Brady through the open door of his class that we were standing in front of.

She rolled her eyes and pushed me towards the door, and I blew her a kiss.

Maybe despite everything, there were still people to trust in the world.

Maybe I should try it again.

4

It was a day like all the rest.
Until it wasn't.

I was in the hallway in front of English literature. Landry had just leaned down to kiss me...when I felt it. An energy so blatant and intense...it was paralyzing.

I froze under Landry's touch, and he pulled back, looking at me questioningly to see what had happened.

But I couldn't drag my attention away from who'd just walked into the building.

It was Jackson.

His eyes were penetrating, narrowed slightly and slowly raking over me, pausing here and there in their perusal... especially where Landry was still touching me.

It had just been a few months, but I'd already been forgetting how beautiful he was. His hair was longer than it had been that night. But it looked even better this length. That gold hair of his fell into his Caribbean blue eyes. My gaze danced from his sculpted cheekbones, to his heart-shaped pout, to the light stubble which accentuated his chiseled face. He was the epitome of primal, raw masculinity.

His expression was fierce...his energy impossible to ignore. Magnetic. Pulling me in.

Landry let out a soft huff of exasperation when he saw Jackson, pulling me closer to him in an act of possession that I wish he'd known was hopeless.

Jackson's body combined with his sculpted face was overkill as it was. But add that to the fact that I knew how that body felt moving inside of me, the fact that just hearing his voice set me on fire, the fact that his soul, although as black as night, called to me the way no one else's ever had?

Landry never had a chance, because my heart couldn't seem to forget that someone else owned it.

Finally, Jackson pulled his gaze from me, leaving me empty inside. I would swear there was a halo of light behind him, accentuating every delectable feature as he walked down the hall. He...laughed at something his football teammate said.

And then he walked right by me, pausing in his stride only once to level me with his focus once more.

His gaze was predatory, and something low inside of me tightened in response. Goosebumps ran along my flesh as he made sure to make contact with me as he passed by. The heat from his body caressed mine.

My heart was beating so wildly, I was afraid that I was going to faint right there. I tried to control my breathing, especially because Landry was still holding me, aware that my heaving chest might be a little too obvious.

I felt exposed, vulnerable...out of control.

What the fuck was wrong with me?

The whole scene only lasted a couple of seconds.

But it was enough to ruin me.

Just like all the other times before.

I wanted to rip my heart out and get a transplant.

Jackson disappeared around the corner, but not before turning his head and giving me a wink that rattled me to my core.

The trouble with time was that it had the unfortunate effect of dulling the edges of the truth you once thought you knew.

I was finally able to turn my attention back to Landry, but the damage had been done. Landry looked furious, his fingers were digging into my waist...and for a second, I was frightened.

A flip seemed to switch in him, the anger fading away until all that was visible was the friendly, devoted, congenial Landry that I'd grown to know so well these past few months.

The rapid change made me churn with unease. "Everything okay, sweetheart?" he asked, and there was no trace in his tone of the venom I'd seen in his face.

"Fine," I responded halfheartedly before trying to step back. His hands tightened even more, and then he released me.

"See you after class, Ev." He strode away without a backwards glance, leaving me even more off kilter with his seemingly blasé reaction to what had happened.

Was my desire for Jackson not written across my face in the way that I thought it was?

I didn't understand.

I COULDN'T CONCENTRATE in class. Jackson's reappearance had shaken me, scared the crap out of me in fact. Was I destined to repeat my same mistakes over and over again, until I was finally burned enough that I was nothing but a pile of ashes?

It seemed that way.

And then there was Landry...that look in his eyes. I'd always had trouble recognizing when the darkness in someone was such that my only choice should be to run.

But that look. It was yelling at me to do just that.

I finally asked to use the restroom and practically ran out of the room, barreling straight into a hard chest.

Looking up, my heart froze.

It was the other face that haunted my dreams. It was Caiden.

I guessed all the monsters that hid under my bed were coming out to play today. I wasn't sure why I hadn't connected it in my head that if Jackson was back in class... then Caiden would be as well. Maybe in an effort to protect myself, my psyche had imagined that even awake, he would be in that hospital room, prevented from ever getting to me.

But here he stood.

If you hadn't known him before, you would never have been able to tell that Caiden had been in a coma. He'd only been awake for around three months, but his physical therapists had done well.

Although slimmer than he had been at the height of his football playing days in high school, he was still a specimen to behold.

A lovely demon I hated with all my being.

Standing here, I thought I would have more guilt.

But honestly, all I could feel was terror.

His hair was longer, shaggier than he'd worn it in high school as well. But it looked intentional, since I could tell that he'd had it freshly cut. He had a ball cap in his hand that he placed carefully on his head, not taking his eyes away from me as he did so. He pulled the cap low over his eyes, shadowing his chiseled face. He looked...older. And bleaker. And just as devastating to my soul.

But not in the way that he used to.

I backed away as he walked towards me tentatively. "LyLy?" he asked, his voice gruffer than I'd remembered it being. Maybe from disuse?

"Get away from me." The words crawled out of my mouth, limping as memories from that night crashed into my skull.

How could he stand there, looking at me somehow like I was everything, after that night?

I'd ruined his life, and he'd ruined mine right back.

"LyLy, what's wrong?" he asked, his voice heavy with confusion. "Why are you acting like this? And why didn't you come visit me in the hospital? I tried to call you a thousand times since I woke up."

"You've got to be fucking kidding me," I hissed, the nonsense coming out of his mouth stopping my retreat as indignation took the place of my fear. "In what world would I ever come see you after what you did to me?"

Of course, I didn't mention all the times I did go see him while he was sleeping.

"What night? The accident? I don't remember any of it." His words came out pleading as he got close to me. I'd forgotten just how much he could express with those dark eyes of his. I'd forgotten the regal slope of his nose, the fullness of his lips. Caiden was beautiful, but it was the kind of beautiful of a poisonous flower you knew would kill you if you touched it.

And I wasn't about to forget that the beauty I was seeing

in front of me was in fact poisonous. Poisonous in a way that I'd never encountered before.

"You don't remember it?" I repeated numbly as the words seeped into my skin.

How convenient. I stared at his eyes, looking for a trace of deception, anything to tell me this was an act.

"I've been told you were in the car with me, that I was going too fast. I know you were injured really bad." Tears filled his gaze as he reached out towards me, and I quickly took a few steps back, convinced that I would burst into ash and desolate ruin if his skin touched mine.

His face filled with hurt at my actions. "I'm so sorry, so fucking sorry. But I feel like me being in a fucking coma for two years should be some kind of penance." The words came out bitter and tired.

And maybe with a rational person that wasn't able to relive every moment of that night...it would have been some kind of penance. But between my memories and my guilt of the damage I'd done to the two people I'd loved most in the world...there wasn't a chance that I could ever let him in again.

"It doesn't matter what you remember or don't remember," I told him somberly. My anger was fading, replaced by sadness at how much had changed that night, how much would always be changed by that night. I'd been alone for the past two years, devoid of anyone that I'd loved.

But I guess, so had he.

"I want you to stay away from me. Whatever was between us is broken, and I have no intention of ever repairing it."

He pulled off his hat and grabbed at his hair, frustrated. "If I don't remember something, how can I fix it?"

I blinked rapidly at him. "There's no fixing anything. I

don't want anything to do with you. I don't want to speak to you. I don't want to see you. Just stay away from me."

I took off down the hallway, running as fast as my ruined leg could take me. It seemed to be hurting even more in his presence, a reminder of that night that would never go away.

"I'll find a way to fix whatever I've done," he called after me.

I shook my head as I slipped into the girls' bathroom, hot tears of shame, fury, and grief streaming down my face.

I'd never thought he'd wake up. Not once in those two years, when I'd sat in that hospital room and apologized over and over again, did I ever think that it would happen.

I'd thought then that I'd do anything if he would just wake up.

But evidently, I had limits. Because doing anything didn't include ever letting Caiden Parker back into my life.

I skipped classes for the rest of the day.

5

The campus was abuzz about the twins' return. Caiden had never been to school here, but he was a legend among the student body, first for his sports' prowess, then for his coma, and now...for his remarkable recovery.

It had been a week, and I felt like I was going mad. He was everywhere. Walking with Jackson, walking with a group of loyal followers he'd already procured, walking too close to me.

The pain of seeing him with Jackson was sharp and aching. Not because their brotherly bond seemed to have been resurrected in the face of his memory loss, but because there had been a time that I'd been right there with them.

Or at least, that's what I tried to tell myself.

If I was being honest with myself, then I would admit that the reason it hurt so bad was because Caiden's presence ensured that Jackson Parker would never be mine again. And even though I'd been the one to push him away...time had been a bitch in reminding me of all his good traits and making me forget why I'd pushed him so far from me that night in the first place.

It also was agonizing because sometimes, I dreamed what it would have been like to have Jackson on my side for the past two years, for him to know what had really happened, and to have been just as hurt and angry on my behalf as he'd been on his brother's behalf when he'd thought that I'd tricked both of them.

I woke up groggily with a dry mouth and the smell of antiseptic burning my nostrils. All I could hear were loud beeps as I tried to figure out what had happened.

An image of Caiden's fist flying towards my face had bile rising up somehow from what must have been an empty stomach. I heard his anger reverberating through the Jeep cabin and felt the sharp pain of bones breaking in my body as he took out his pain on me. I remembered him ripping through the streets, the downpour of rain beating on the roof. I remembered the panic and then the crash of metal breaking and bending.

We'd been in an accident. Caiden had beat the shit out of me after finding out about Jackson and I.

I tried to move, and pain sliced through me. Only then did I become truly aware of the situation I was in. Bandages covered my whole body. My leg was in a heavy cast. Wires and tubes extended out of me everywhere.

I began to cry, dry, racking sobs. Was Caiden all right? Did he look like me right now?

And where was Jackson?

I'd been alone plenty in my life. I'd accepted it in fact as a permanent part of my life, even with the presence of the twins. But I'd never felt as alone as I did right now, waking up in this hospital room, with injuries that I knew must be severe, completely and utterly by myself.

I let myself feel the pain for a few minutes, and then I pressed the nurse button on the side of the bed, even that small act sending shockwaves of hurt through my ribs from the movement.

A few seconds passed, and then a plump, sweet looking nurse with grey streaked, chestnut brown hair came barreling into the room. She was slightly out of breath from the effort, and the smile on her face sent me over the edge. I started to cry again, this time, even harder.

"Oh darlin', let it all out. I know this is difficult, sweetheart. I know. But you're going to be as right as rain in no time. We've been working round the clock to bring you back to the land of the living."

"How long have I been asleep?" I asked, my words coming out fractured and garbled because of the tubes they'd had in my mouth while I was sleeping.

"Let's work on getting you some water to help your throat, and then we can talk all about everything," she told me hurriedly. "Don't talk anymore until we get that out, okay. I don't want it to cause any more swelling to your throat."

I nodded when she gave me an expectant look. My nod launched her into action, and soon there was a whole team of nurses and doctors standing around me, fiddling with tubes in my arms and mercifully removing the feeding tube that had been down my throat. Apparently at one time, I'd been on oxygen due to my collapsed lung, but that had gotten better sometime in the last week.

I'd been asleep for a week.

"Have you talked to my mom? Has she been here?" I asked Cecilia, that first nurse that had come into my room.

Her gaze shifted nervously around the room. "We've been in contact with her, keeping her updated every day."

"She hasn't been here?" I didn't know why I sounded so disappointed. In what world had my mother ever cared about me?

"She was here on the first day. I think it was too hard seeing you like that. It was a bit touch and go there for a minute there, baby cakes." The nurse still didn't make eye contact with me.

I sighed. "You don't have to cover for her. I wouldn't have expected anything different." Then I remembered something important. *"And Caiden? How is he?"* I asked, realizing that should have been the first thing I'd asked instead of descending into a pity party that I didn't deserve.

"His injuries were a lot less than yours," she said quietly. *"But an incident happened, and he's been in a coma since then."*

"An incident?"

She shook her head somberly. "I'm sorry, I can't tell you more. We're all just praying that he wakes up. This has been an enormous tragedy for our town."

I didn't say anything to that. If the town was mourning, it definitely wasn't because of me. If only I had been hurt, there would probably be a parade through the center of town that one less James was alive on this planet.

I needed answers. A coma? An incident? My brain was exhausted, despite the fact that I'd been asleep for the last week. I drifted into dreamland, a land where the burning fumes of the crash and the tortured screams of Caiden were all you could find.

When I woke up, I wasn't alone. I'd always been able to feel Jackson's presence. It was impossible to miss, so overwhelming and all-encompassing that I wasn't sure if I was actually noticed at all by other people if he was in the vicinity.

He was standing there by the door, leaning against the wall as he just watched me.

Jackson.

It was like my soul let out a sigh of relief with his presence.

I wasn't alone.

He didn't say anything.

"You're here," I finally said.

Still nothing.

"How's Caiden?" I asked desperately. *"The nurses wouldn't say anything."*

The mention of his twin's name seemed to spark Jackson to life.

A low bitter laugh sounded out of his beautiful mouth. Sparks flickered down my spine. I should have known that his dark laugh was a warning shot for the destruction he was about to wreak.

Evidently, the twins were both good about destroying fragile, broken things.

I still didn't see it coming.

"How's Caiden?" he repeated mockingly. "That's rich coming from you."

My cruel, beautiful boy leveled me with a look I'd only seen him give his worst enemies.

"Caiden told me everything," Jackson said in a low voice etched with arsenic and madness.

I was confused. If Caiden had told him everything, why was he acting like this?

I opened my mouth and then closed it, not sure what to say.

"I have to admit, you're a better actress than I thought possible, Everly. I mean, you even acted like it hurt when I first pushed in. Just like a fucking virgin would."

"I was a virgin," I said slowly, hurt creeping up my veins.

He did that laugh again, the one that made me sore and troubled. The one that spelled trouble for me. "Right. Was it a bet you had with someone, or was it just a game you were playing with yourself? Get both the Parker boys to fuck you and fall in love with you. Did you still have his cum in you as you stood at my door and convinced me to break my brother's heart?"

I gaped in horror at him. What exactly had Caiden told him?

"Caiden's lying in a fucking hospital bed, most likely never to wake up again because of you. He tried to kill himself rather than exist in a world with you and I, Everly. How does that make you feel? Do you feel good about yourself? Does that give you the *affirmation you need because of what your bastard dad and mom did to you?"*

Tears were choking my throat. I didn't know what to address first. Caiden had tried to kill himself? Why would he do that?

Jackson's words were a whip that slashed through me over and over again, until I wasn't sure how I wasn't bleeding out all over the hospital bed right then.

"They don't think he'll wake up?" I finally asked, dazed at everything coming out right now.

"No. And it's all your fault."

"Jackson, I never—"

"Save it for someone who doesn't know you're a liar, Everly James. It should be you in that coma, not him," Jackson spat, and then he left the room without a look back. His parting words were like knife wounds to my chest.

I clawed at my skin as my body overheated. I'd been sipping liquids the last two days since I'd woken up, and all of it came wrenching out of my mouth, covering the front of my hospital gown in a pathetic display of a girl who'd lost everything... including possibly her mind.

I let out a high-pitched wail as my blood pressure sensor went off, alerting anyone in the vicinity of my distress.

The same rosy-cheeked nurse came in, took one look at me, and then grabbed a syringe off one of the machines.

"Everything will be better tomorrow, my sweet," she promised falsely as she injected the syringe into one of my IV lines.

Right away, the world started to get blurry and the pain dulled.

I wish I could sleep forever, I thought.

But I didn't think forever would be enough to erase the agony of what had just occurred.

I was truly all alone now.

I was brought back to the present by Lane squealing about the new top she'd found for the hockey party on Friday that was going to go great with the pink in her hair. I smiled mechanically, wondering if there was a way that I could get out of it and not hurt Landry's feelings.

I mean, he was my boyfriend, right? Even if our relationship had consisted of a lot of study sessions and very few make-out sessions. If I didn't feel like going, it shouldn't be a big deal, as long as I was at the game cheering him on and wearing his jersey. And I would be. I wasn't that much of a selfish bastard to disappoint him by getting out of the game, even if I'd heard that the whole football team plus Caiden—because I'd heard he was going to be on the team in the fall—would be at the game, cheering on the hockey team.

"Landry, you'd be okay if I just went back to my room after the game, right?" I tentatively asked, cutting off the conversation that Lane and Landry were having with one another.

"You don't want to come to the party?" both Lane and he said at almost the same time.

"I'm honestly dreading it. With everything that has happened this semester, I have a crazy amount of anxiety about it."

Landry's face tightened. He grabbed at his russet hair, agitated. "Ev, I don't know what's going on with you, but I feel like you're never here with me anymore. I'm honestly not okay with you peacing out on the party," he spat, throwing my words back in my face. "It's important to me to have my girlfriend there."

My heart tightened with his use of the term "girlfriend."

I just so happened to look up and see Jackson and Caiden laughing with each other and their adoring fans.

I needed to do better. I needed to move on. Landry was offering me that chance, despite how much I put him through. I mean, I'd fucked Jackson in the bathroom on our first date. And still, he was here.

I couldn't let this slip out of my fingertips by pining away for something I couldn't have.

6

"We Will Rock You" pounded through the speakers of the ice arena. The team was on fire tonight, especially Landry. I was decked for the game in his number twenty-eight jersey, and the sight seemed to have given him an extra push. He already had a hat trick tonight, and the team was up 3-0 because of it.

The song faded away as the whole arena began to chant "Evans" over and over again while Landry lined up to take a penalty shot.

When it went in, the whole place exploded. It was 4-0 now, and assuming our goalie didn't have a massive record-breaking meltdown in these last three minutes, the championship was ours.

My gaze flicked away from the game to where the football team was sitting across the way.

It was just my luck that two burning gazes were already focused on me. Jackson and Caiden were standing next to some of the offensive linemen, who'd come to the game with giant letters spelling out "Go Team" on their enormous bellies. The fans couldn't get enough of them, but I could only focus on the two men beside them.

As soon as I saw them looking at me, I pulled my gaze back to the game, my nerves spiking from their attention.

I'd been sneaking looks at them all game. Jackson had looked bored, clearly not caring at all to be there, while Caiden had looked like he was having the time of his life, laughing and cheering it up with his soon to be teammates.

He looked healthier than ever, like coming to school had infused him with the extra energy he needed to make that last step of recovering. I was sure that his muscles were still not even close to recovering after lying dormant for two years, besides the manual ministrations given to him daily by a physical therapist, but here, under the lights of the hockey arena...he sure looked recovered.

I was keeping my eye on the snake in the grass, yes, but most of my attention—when it wasn't focused on the game and Landry of course—was on Jackson.

And judging by the amount of time he'd spent staring at me during the game, most of his attention was on me as well.

I couldn't breathe.

"I'm going to get some popcorn. Want anything?" I asked Lane, who was similarly clad in a jersey from another member of the hockey team that she'd been hooking up with over the last month. I'd heard way too many details about the goalie's dick size and his prowess in the sack to ever be able to look him in the eye again.

"We only have three minutes left... You can't wait?" she asked, raising her brow quizzically as the crowd cheered a block by her lover.

"Girl's got to eat," I lied, and she rolled her eyes, seeing right through me.

Heartbreak Lover

I walked out of our aisle at the bottom of the arena, right by the glass, and walked briskly up the stairs. I hovered in front of the concession stand before deciding that my stomach was in too many knots for me to eat. Hurrying around the corner where there were no people, I leaned against the wall, taking a deep sigh of relief about escaping the constant gazes that seemed to follow me everywhere lately.

I felt him then, and even before I opened my eyes, I knew that Jackson would be standing right in front of me as soon as I did.

Sure enough, as my eyes opened...there he was.

We didn't say anything, and I took a moment to analyze his features. The way his golden hair whisked across his forehead made me want to brush my fingers across it. His eyes gleamed like cobalt-colored jewels, no sign of the black that haunted my dreams in their depths. He had a five o'clock shadow, making him look edgy and older than his years. I imagined myself dragging my tongue across that plump lower lip and feeling the prickles of the overgrown stubble as I did so.

Jackson's gaze stayed pinned on mine, and it felt like he could read every one of my lustful thoughts. He called to me, like always. And just like always...I was powerless against his pull.

A tremble ran through me at his intense gaze. It burned over my skin as we looked at each other. His eyes glimmered with intensity, and I licked my lips in response, causing him to jerk at the movement.

He moved towards me then, hauling me towards him with one hand while he cradled my neck with his other large hand. I inhaled and craned my head to the opposite side, offering my sensitive skin for his taking, even if my brain was screaming at me to run away. The move was instinctual. His hand glided down my neck, over my shoulder, as his fingertips trailed featherlight along my arm. Jackson's eyes were dark and hooded as they zeroed in on my mouth. His pink tongue barely jutted out to wet perfectly plump lips. Goosebumps spread along my arm. His hand stopped at my wrist, and he caressed the pulse point there slowly, almost as if he was tracing letters against my skin. Over and over.

The action made me twitchy, needy...on edge.

I was about to ask him why he'd followed me when he pressed his body against me suddenly, pinning me against the wall. A protest sat on the edge of my lips until his mouth prevented any speech. The moment our lips touched, it was magic...just like all the times before.

I lost all thought. His fingers entwined with mine, palm to palm. Electricity sizzled between our clasped hands as he held them over my head, pressing his large, warm body against mine. The power behind his kiss, the wet heat, fingers clutching, chest pinning me to the wall, was exhilarating. It was like a car, racing towards the finish line, going the distance and crossing in an explosion of excitement.

The forbidden nature of his passion had my mind in a drunken tizzy. The realization that I was allowing him to control me just like all the times before was a bitter pill to swallow...but it felt too good to stop.

His lips nibbled and plucked, and a delicious sensation ricocheted through every pore as sparks of lust raced through me.

I needed more. Of him. Of his mouth. Of his body against mine.

Just more.

I sucked his tongue greedily, and I was rewarded with

him returning my fervor with a kiss somehow even more scorching than all the ones before. He pressed closer to me as if he was trying to attach himself to me, and tingles of pleasure rippled out from his touch.

Jackson kissed his way down my neck, and I was lost in the sensation. His familiar scent of sandalwood and frankincense washed over me, settling into my senses. It was intoxicating, pulling me further into the abyss that was all things Jackson. I trembled with need, my breath ragged as I gripped and clawed at him, trying to pull him deeper against me, to merge us as one.

His lips brushed my ear, sending more chills pitter-pattering across my skin. I heard his intake of breath as he dragged his warm tongue down the column of my neck, tasting, devouring. He moaned and bit down hard on the space between my shoulder and my neck. Excitement at his claim built between my thighs, moisture pooling and soaking my underwear.

The way he took control of me and my body, I didn't think it could be replicated. I'd certainly never felt it with the other two boys I'd kissed in my life. I inhaled again, creepily wanting to bottle his scent and spray it on every surface I touched so I could experience it all the time.

It was both frightening and freeing to have this kiss with him, as if I'd been a dam about to break all these months and he'd just given me permission to break through my stone walls. I wanted to beg for more and run for fear...all at the same time.

"Wow, sorry Jackson," a voice rumbled as someone came around the corner and saw us before hurrying back where he'd come from.

It was like water had been thrown over me, the realization of what we'd just done sinking into me until all I could feel was guilt and disgust.

Just then an enormous cheer swelled out from the crowd as the buzzer sounded, signaling the end of the game.

Landry.

I was destined to fuck up everything in my life. And it was always because of my inability to resist Jackson's call.

"I've got to go," I told him, pushing him away. He looked just as shell-shocked as I imagined I did over what had just happened. It was like this thing between us was too much to possibly be ignored.

"You have to get back to Landry," he growled, the sound setting my insides aflutter with lust, even as guilt over my actions battled for supremacy.

"We're dating," I told him, and I hated how it sounded apologetic coming out of my mouth.

"He's telling everyone that you're his girlfriend."

"I think that's none of your business."

We stared at each other until another cheer told me I'd lingered for too long. I ran away, feeling his hot gaze licking along my spine the entire time.

People were still hugging each other and celebrating loudly when I found my way back to my seat. "We won!" Lane cried as she jumped at me, encompassing me in a warm hug I didn't think I deserved.

She sniffed and pushed away from me. "You didn't!" she practically yelled, sounding strangely not disappointed in me.

"Did what?" I asked, trying to sound innocent. Lane's gaze flicked over to where Jackson was just sitting down in his seat again, Caiden questioning him about something with a frown on his face.

"I'm supposed to believe it's just a coincidence that you came back smelling like Jackson and sex at the same time as him? Girl, y'all's hair was not that rumpled before you left. And I was watching him, the second you got out of your seat and left, he was like a bat out of hell hustling up those stairs."

I pulled on the bottom of my hair, near tears. "We didn't have sex. Also, how do you know what Jackson smells like?" I commented defensively.

She rolled her eyes. "I couldn't help but take a sniff a time or two as he passed by, I'm only human."

I sighed and ran a stressed and guilty hand across my face.

"Oh honey...this is a good thing," she cooed softly as she patted my arm.

"But Landry..."

She scoffed. "I know I've given you a hard time, but Landry knew the deal when he started after you. He knew you and Jackson were something, and he still didn't give up. He knows you and Jackson are complicated, and yet he still is trying to be all up in your business. Frankly...it's fucking annoying."

I stare at her, shocked. I'd always thought that she liked Landry, that she was rooting for him.

"I'm just not convinced that the good guy is who you're supposed to end up with in this story," she told me with a shrug. She caught Jackson looking at me again and leveled him with a saucy wave. His eyebrows rose in surprise, and I could tell he didn't know if he was supposed to respond or not.

The awkward moment was so unlike Jackson that I couldn't help but laugh.

It felt good to laugh.

I didn't know if Lane was right or not about Landry, but it sure helped to absolve some of my guilt.

"I need to tell Landry tonight, regardless," I told her, looking over to where the hockey team was proudly hoisting the championship trophy up high.

She grabbed my shoulders. "No you do not. Why can't you have fun while you figure all this crap out? Besides...he just won the championship, let's not douse his hopes and dreams by telling him that the hottie he's obsessed with was making out with his arch-rival at the end of the game and missed his final goal."

My cheeks blazed scarlet, I could feel my blush heating up my neck and cheeks as it spread.

"He called me his girlfriend the other day," I reminded her.

She rolled her eyes. "I didn't hear you acknowledge it or call him boyfriend, babe. Trust me...Landry knows the score."

I eyed her suspiciously.

"What do you know?" She pretended to look innocent, and I realized how laughable it was when I tried that same face on her. "Lane..."

"Tony may have mentioned that Landry had talked about it," she finally said with a shrug. Tony was her goalie fling.

"What did he say?" I demanded.

"He just was ranting about how you'd acted when you saw Jackson the other day. He told Tony he was going to do everything he could to keep you but that Jackson would fight dirty."

She shrugged as if what she was saying was no big deal. "Tony asked him if he thought you were fucking Jackson, and he said he didn't care if you were, that eventually, he would win you over."

My mouth dropped.

"So you see, that was a good thing. He knows he's got to work for it, and he's willing to."

"I'm not this kind of girl," I grumbled.

Lane laughed and patted me on my back. "It's okay, little baby. Auntie Lane will help you play in the dark side."

I smacked her hand away playfully, just as a bang sounded on the glass.

It was a euphoric looking Landry, adorably sweaty and mussed from his game. "We did it," he yelled, and Lane and I whooped and hollered as expected. "See you in a few hours at the party?" he asked as one of his teammates skated to him and began to pull on his jersey to get him back with the still celebrating team.

Just like every time the party was mentioned, a wave of unease flickered around in my gut. But I smiled and gave him a thumbs up, watching nervously as he skated away.

"We'll have fun tonight. Just you wait!" Lane announced excitedly as she began to pull me towards the stairs.

I cast one last look back behind me, my gaze catching on a hungry-looking Jackson. Always looking at me.

But so was Caiden.

7

The party was in full swing as we made our way through the giant double doors of the hockey fraternity. We were about an hour later than planned, thanks to Lane begging to do my hair and makeup, and everyone looked like they were already plastered.

I saw some members of the football team as we passed through the front room, and I elbowed Lane. "The football team's here!"

She looked at me like I was an idiot. "Babe, everyone's here. Good thing you look fucking hot."

I could admit that she was right. I did look "fucking hot."

Lane had curled my long blonde hair into beach waves, and I had a white bandage dress on that molded to my every curve. I was on the lookout for Melanie to appear from a dark corner and throw a cup of red punch all over it. Because it looked damn good.

Lane had applied a shimmering gold eyeshadow to my eyelids and lined my eyes with kohl black eyeliner and three coats of mascara, accentuating the green of them. She'd had a goal to have all eyes on her and I tonight, and judging by the looks we were getting...she had succeeded.

Lane looked gorgeous. She was wearing a bubblegum pink halter top that showed off her toned stomach and a black mini skirt. Her pink-streaked hair was up in a sexy, mussed up high pony that accentuated her long neck. Sky high black heels completed the look.

When I'd first met Lane, I'd never thought she'd be caught dead in such an outfit, but I had quickly learned that Lane was a rebel without a cause. She didn't stick to any of the prescribed social boundaries that anyone else deigned to place her in. I loved it.

"There's Landry," she said pointing to a group of hockey players playing flip cup. There were at least fifteen gorgeous girls vying for their attention, and it really said something for my current feelings when I was disappointed that Landry was acting like they didn't exist.

I went to make my way over to him, but Lane stopped me. "Let's go dance for a while. Eventually, Tony and Landry will hear about the hot girls making waves on the dance floor and figure out that it's us," she said with a wink before dragging me down the basement steps to where a DJ was cranking out Top 40 hits for the crowd of sweaty, writhing college students paying homage to him on the dance floor.

Lane began to dance around me to her own beat...as was her way. I began to move my hips, awkwardly at first and then more smoothly as I let the beat of the Chainsmokers' song carry me. Guys tried to step into our circle and get up on us, but we politely pushed them away. Lane procured drinks for us out of seemingly thin air, and we quickly got buzzed on cheap vodka punch and thumping beats.

I was lost in the moment when Jackson appeared at the

bottom of the stairs, his gaze gliding around the room as if he was looking for me.

"Heartbreak prince on aisle two," Lane announced rather loudly as she shimmied to the Rihanna song that just started.

I shh'd her, a little too buzzed to really care about her loudness though.

And then he was there, his hands caressing my sides possessively as his hard chest and stomach pressed against me, pinning me to him. He bent forward, allowing our hips to align perfectly, and a low moan hissed out of my lips as I felt him start to harden behind me at my touch.

"You look like pure sin wrapped in an angelic package," he murmured harshly into my ear, his hot breath gusting over the side of my face as his lips grazed the outer shell of my ear as he spoke. Everything else around us, the music and the drunken laughter and shouting...it all faded away at his touch. My pulse raced, and my lips parted as I let out panting breaths.

His fingers tightened, digging into my hips, and unlike the fear I felt when Landry had done almost the same thing, his possessive hold just filled me with lust. "I've given you time, little angel. I've let you have your fun. But I'm done waiting. I'm coming to collect."

His words were confusing...and hot as he moved seductively with me to a song all about sex and desire.

I probably should have been looking for Landry. I probably should have pushed him away.

I probably should have done a lot of things.

But I just moved with him.

His long fingers fanned out across my hips and lower stomach, pressing me more firmly into his body, molding me to him. His large biceps caged my arms, and he brushed

Heartbreak Lover

his nose down the side of my neck. I remembered his bite at the hockey game, a bruise that I had to cover in order to wear this dress, and crazily craved more.

He turned me around, and I got a better look at him. He was wearing a midnight blue Henley, unbuttoned at the top, showing off the indents of his perfect chest. *A chest that tasted delicious*, I drunkenly reminded myself. The color of his shirt accentuated his beautiful eyes. And his black jeans and his black boots accentuated everything else.

I groaned inwardly at how good he looked.

Or at least, I thought I said it silently until he gave me a smug look.

He looked dangerous and wild, and I needed someone to remind me why this was such a bad idea. He leaned forward to kiss me, and then, over his shoulder, I saw Caiden coming down the stairs, his gaze also scanning the crowd as if he was looking for someone...just like his brother.

Freezing, I came to my senses and pushed Jackson away. Surprise was written all over his face, he obviously thought he had me. But there was no better reminder of why Jackson and I couldn't be together than the sight of Caiden.

Ducking away from Jackson, who called out after me, I weaved my way through the crowd, staying on the opposite side of the room from Caiden.

Once at the entryway, I sneaked a look back at a furious-looking Jackson and a confused-looking Lane, and then I booked it up the stairs.

The first floor was packed even more than when we'd first arrived, and I felt like a panic attack was coming on as people bumped me and touched me as I passed by. Seeing a gap by the stairs that led to the second floor, I stumbled up them, thinking I could recover in the bathroom.

There were couples making out in the long hallway, and in one of the rooms I tried, there was an actual orgy happening with three girls and a very happy member of the hockey team, whose face would be scarred in my memory for forever after what I'd seen.

I finally found a blissfully empty bathroom, and I slammed the door, locking it behind me as I took deep breaths, trying to calm down.

What was I doing? I wanted to claw my insides out, get a new heart that wouldn't be as defective as the one currently residing in my chest. I beat on my chest savagely, trying to knock some sense into me.

I wanted to cry. Because it felt so hopeless to think I might never be done with this wild, destructive thing between Jackson and I.

A few more deep breaths, and I'd decided to find Lane and Landry and tell them I was going to go. Crowds weren't my thing, and combined with Landry, Jackson...and Caiden, it was too much.

I slipped out into the hallway, bypassing a couple that was actually having sex against the wall, and took a step down the first step.

I heard footsteps suddenly behind me, and before I could turn my head to look, a pair of hands pushed on my back firmly, sending me hurtling down the stairs with a wide, silent scream on my lips.

The first hit to my head sent stars spiraling across my vision, but the second and third hits were what really did me in. I felt like something cracked in my leg as I did another nasty tumble, and then the world went blissfully dark.

"Everly!" a voice called out frantically. I tried to open my eyes, but I only saw blurs in front of me. My eyes began to close again, and then I heard Lane's voice calling my name. She sounded so...scared.

It's okay Lane, I tried to speak, but the words didn't seem to want to come out.

"She's waking up!" a voice yelled a little too close to my ear, and I groaned as it made my head hurt even worse.

Once more, I tried to open my eyes. Blearily, I realized that a group of guys were kneeled around me along with a terrified looking Lane.

"Everly," she cried out when she saw that my eyes were open. She pounced on me, and I gave a small moan because my leg and my head were killing me.

"Get off her," Jackson barked, and I realized that he was one of the kneeling figures. As was Landry. As was Caiden.

I scrambled to move away from Caiden and let out a low hiss as the movement sent another shock of pain through my leg and head.

"Get away from me," I told Caiden. His eyes widened. Something that looked a lot like anger flashed through them before hurt masked any other emotion.

"It's just Caiden, Everly," Jackson soothed, confusion in his gaze as he looked from me to his brother.

I dragged my attention away from Caiden...and Jackson, and focused on Lane and Landry.

"What happened?" I asked as I tried to sit up.

"Don't move," Lane begged. I looked at her questioningly.

"They never let the main character move when they fall in the movies," she explained seriously, garnering incredulous stares from everyone gathered around.

"I'm sitting up," I said firmly, right as a crew of first

responders came marching through the front door of the frat house...with a gurney.

"Please no," I groaned as the team gathered around me.

It took a minute to realize just how much pain I was in though. Something was definitely wrong with my leg. Hot tears started to fall when I thought of how much I'd already been through to get my leg working again.

I was hoisted onto the gurney, what felt like a million people's gazes locked on my every move. Landry was by my side as I was wheeled out, but as I looked back...Jackson just looked lost. He looked like he'd just come to a terrible realization, but I couldn't figure out what it was.

And Caiden...he was just watching me leave. A grim look on his face.

8

At the hospital, I waited for the bad news. Landry had told everyone he was my boyfriend so that he could stay with me, and I didn't have the strength or energy to correct him. Lane had taken a cab to the hospital and had somehow managed to beg her way into my room, probably telling the staff she was my sister or something so that she would be allowed access.

As soon as the doctor left after his initial checkup, Landry whirled around, a furious look on his face. "Why didn't you come find me as soon as you guys got to the party? And how much did you fucking drink? I can't believe you fell down the stairs, you aren't even wearing heels."

I knew he was just concerned, but I was annoyed at his tone. "I didn't 'fall' down the stairs, Landry. I was pushed."

Lane gasped, putting her hand over her mouth.

"Are you sure?" Landry asked, a note of doubt laced through his voice.

I got irrationally angry. "I told you I shouldn't have come. You know that someone's been doing something to me.

They obviously took advantage of the crowd to get close to me once again."

"It wouldn't have happened if you hadn't been off doing who knows what at the party," Landry spit out. He grabbed at his hair. "Fuck. I didn't mean that."

"I think you should probably go home. Lane's here, and I'll be fine," I told him stiffly, trying to keep my upper lip from quivering too much.

Landry sighed heavily. He opened his mouth to argue, but Lane must have shot him a look behind my back, because he promptly snapped his mouth closed without saying anything.

"Will you call me with how you're doing?" he asked desperately as he hovered by the door.

"I'll text you," I said firmly with my best "fuck you" voice.

Landry looked like I'd kicked his puppy as he walked out of the room. I couldn't find it in myself to care.

"I'm sorry too," said Lane in a small voice as she came and sat on the edge of my hospital bed, tears brimming in her eyes. They were red-rimmed and swollen. I don't think she'd stopped crying since I'd woken up.

"What are you sorry for?"

"I shouldn't have pushed you to go to the party. You're just already so closed off. I just wanted you to have fun."

"I didn't want to go to the party because I was scared, I just didn't want to be around Jackson, if he showed up...and I hate crowds," I admitted, not wanting her to feel bad for something she didn't do.

She laid her head on my shoulder. I hated hospitals, and I was scared to death of what the doctors were going to come back and say about my leg, but it was nice to have someone with me for once.

It seemed to take forever, but the doctor finally came

into the room. My heart skipped around in my chest as I waited for the news. His face was perfectly blank, and it was impossible to get a read on him.

"You, Ms. James, are a lucky girl. You have a concussion, and a bad contusion on your shoulder, but you only have a bruised bone on your leg. You'll need to be on crutches for two weeks, but I expect you to be back to normal after that."

My relief was palpable, and the doctor's gaze warmed as he looked at me. "I know you've been through a lot these last few years after I looked through your records, Everly. But this particular hard thing will be over before you know it."

I nodded, unable to speak, because I didn't want to cry anymore. Lane was doing enough crying for both of us.

"Do you have anyone who can stay with you tonight and make sure to wake you up every couple of hours to make sure you're all right?" the doctor asked.

"I will," came Jackson's voice from the doorway, causing all of us to jump from the unexpectedness of it.

Lane immediately jumped to the rescue. "She can stay with me."

"You have a roommate and a twin bed, you can't fit someone else. It's just me in my place, and I have a queen size bed and couch," Jackson argued calmly, as if it didn't matter one way or another to him what happened and he was just stating facts.

The doctor looked between Lane and Jackson awkwardly. "Well, I'll just let you decide, dear," he finally said to me, patting my good knee before he walked towards the doorway. "The nurse will be in soon with your papers, and then you can go. Good luck, Ms. James."

I was tempted to call for him to come back with the way Lane and Jackson were eyeing one another.

"She's not going to get better sleeping on the floor of your dorm," Jackson snarled at Lane.

Lane looked affronted. "I would give her my bed!"

"I'll go with Jackson," I said tiredly, wanting a bed desperately. Lane's roommate wasn't the friendliest, although she was no Melanie, and I didn't want Lane to have any more problems with her because of my presence.

Lane looked shocked. "Can I talk to you...privately?" she asked when Jackson showed no hint of leaving.

The nurse came in just then, preventing any conversations I was too tired to deal with. Five minutes later, and I was on my way...Jackson and Lane bickering the whole way to Jackson's enormous truck.

"It's okay guys, I just need to sleep," I finally told them when they showed no signs of stopping.

Lane huffed. "I'm going to ask her all about what happens tonight, buddy. So you better play nice," she snarled at Jackson.

Jackson rolled his eyes like she was being ridiculous. Time must have taken the edge off of his memories as well.

Moments later, I was in the passenger seat of Jackson's truck, a place I'd never imagined myself sitting again.

"Thanks for this," I told him nervously.

He huffed like I'd just said something ridiculous.

We didn't say anything else the entire drive back to his place.

The truck pulled into a townhome community about a mile beyond campus. It was brand new, judging by the fact that half of it was still under construction.

"This is nice," I commented lamely.

He just nodded. We pulled into the garage, and my brain sparked to life.

"Does Caiden live here too?" I panicked just thinking

about him being nearby. There was no way that I could sleep with him here. For some reason, my fear of him had been growing, despite the fact that we hadn't spoken since that first day in the hallway. It was like the less I talked to him, the more of the bogeyman he became.

It was just another thing I should probably get therapy about.

I opened the door, prepared to jump out despite the fact that I would have to somehow get home with a concussion and crutches. I was prepared to do it if it meant getting away though. My concussion must be pretty bad for me to have even agreed to come here in the first place.

As soon as I stepped a foot out of the truck, a wave of dizziness hit me.

"What the hell are you doing?" Jackson snarled as I heard his driver-side door slam closed and his hurried footsteps approach.

"Baby, what are you doing?" he asked again, and this time, his voice was gentle and comforting. He embraced me, his strong arms enveloping me suddenly. Warm and safe. I'd forgotten what it felt like. I breathed in his scent, letting myself be weak because my head fucking hurt.

He pulled me closer to him, and I leaned against his chest and listened to his heartbeat. It should calm and soothe me, but it did the opposite of that. Tears began to stream down my face, wetting his shirt. Deep gut-wrenching sobs spilled out of me as I let all the stress of this semester out, even though he'd been the cause of much of the stress. Jackson's arms held me tight.

"Sweet angel, I've got you," he breathed. "I'm right here." He stroked my hair.

Am I dreaming? I must be dreaming. Because in what world am I at Jackson's place, and he's comforting me?

Caiden.

The fear hit me again, and I pushed away before realizing that Jackson's truck was the only vehicle in the garage.

"Caiden wanted to live on campus," Jackson said slowly. "And I just moved to this place last week. I live alone."

I looked at him through watery eyes. He stared down at me with that same inscrutable expression that he'd had at the frat house. Like he'd figured something out.

The pain medication they filled me with started to take effect, and I slumped against him. He swooped me up in his arms, my crutches clattering to the garage floor. I kept my eyes closed as we walked, my eyes too tired to take a look at his place. We went up a set of stairs, and then moments later, I was on a big, soft bed.

Jackson began to inch up my dress, and I groaned. When I made no move to help him, he laid me back down onto his pillow, and he walked to his dresser, proceeding to take off his watch and set it on top. I watched as if through a fog as he pulled his Henley over his head.

I let out a soft gasp because the pain medicine seemed to have taken away all my inhibitions. His body was still the stuff of dreams. It was incredible, tall with broad muscled shoulders that narrowed into a tight chest, lean waist, and hips. My mouth watered just looking at him. There was a slight smirk on his lips that told me he knew I was salivating, but he thankfully said nothing. He slipped out of his jeans, leaving him in nothing but a tight pair of grey briefs that showed everything.

And I mean everything.

Which made me think about his cock. I could tell it was semi-erect, and in my drugged-out state, all I could think about was falling to my knees and wrapping my lips around the perfect head in complete adoration of its beauty.

Again, I obviously hit my head hard.

Jackson adjusted himself unabashedly, and then pulled the covers away on the other side of the bed, proceeding to get in.

"What are you doing?" I all but shrieked as I dragged my gaze away from his dick and to his still smirking, freakishly gorgeous lips.

"I'm going to bed. You said you were tired." His voice was amused, as if he was privy to a joke that I wasn't a part of.

"You told Lane there was a couch."

"There is a couch, but it's not nearly as comfortable as my bed."

I tried to sit up to get out of the bed and immediately sank back down as the room spun around me.

Jackson brought his face close to mine and trailed featherlight touches down the side of my face. He brushed a kiss against my forehead, and a traitorous tear fell down my cheek. Why was he being so sweet to me? I had no defense against this version of Jackson. This version made me forget how much of an asshole he was. I shivered from the feel of his mouth against mine and snuggled deeper into the bed that was a thousand times more comfortable than my dorm bed.

"Sleep, little angel. I'll wake you every couple of hours, just as the doctor ordered."

I was already fading into dreamland before he finished speaking, lost in his scent that surrounded me in his sheets and pillows.

Keeping his word, Jackson woke me up two hours later. His soft, soothing fingers caressed my face and hairline, bringing me out of the good dream I was having.

A dream about him of course. Because what else would I dream about?

My eyes flickered open, and I met his half-hooded gaze. His eyes looked more of a midnight blue in the dim lighting. The muted glow of the lamp he'd turned on made me feel like we were in our own little cocoon. His features were relaxed and open. I could almost see the boy that I'd grown up with in his face.

He held up an ice pack. "We should put this on your head for a little bit." I moaned when he pressed it against me, sending shivers all over my skin.

"Everly, where are you?" he asked in a hushed voice.

"Your place," I responded groggily. The pain medication they'd given me made it feel like I was talking through a mouth full of cotton.

"Good girl," he said as he reached over to the black nightstand next to him and grabbed the pill bottle they'd given us at the hospital. He emptied two pills out into his hand and handed them to me along with a small cup of water. "Take these."

I sleepily gulped them down and then burrowed back into the bed. He put the glass back down on the table and then pulled the covers back over me after taking away the ice pack. The lamp was switched off after that, leaving the room bathed in the soft moonlight.

He laid back down and stared at me intently, studying every feature of my face.

I smiled back softly in response, the pain medicine obviously making me out of my head. He was so fucking gorgeous.

"Thanks, little angel," he said, amusement threaded throughout his gravelly, sleep-laden voice.

I hadn't meant to say that out loud. Obviously.

"I kind of figured that."

Fuck.

Jackson suddenly planted a soft kiss against my lips. He cradled my face gently, as if I was made of glass, and I returned the kiss as he slid his perfect lips against mine.

His assault on my mouth was slow, unhurried, like he had all the time in the world. He didn't increase the pressure or try to take it further. It was tortuous.

And perfect.

Just like him.

I could imagine us doing this for the rest of our lives right in this moment. It was dangerous territory for my already destroyed heart. He stroked my bottom lip with his tongue, and I slid my fingers into his hairline, increasing the pressure as I begged him for more. Evidently, that was all the permission he needed, because he began to take my mouth greedily, his mouth threatening to swallow me whole. His tongue swept past my teeth and against my tongue in long unhurried swipes.

A moan left me, unbidden. He tasted so good. It was like his taste was manufactured by the gods to be exactly what tasted best to me, exactly what I needed. I wanted his body on top of me, coating every surface with his warm skin.

I tugged at his shoulders and attempted to bring him against my chest.

It didn't work.

He was unmovable above me. I wound my legs between his in order to aid in my goal.

When Jackson pulled away, a stark cry flew out of my mouth.

"Why?" I asked desperately.

He moaned before his large hand slipped under my dress and began to trace the edge of my panties. My breath puffed out in tiny frantic bursts of excitement from the heat of his head at the base of my neck, his five o'clock shadow grating along the skin there. He nibbled a line from my chin to my mouth. Once he reached my mouth, I took his lips in a feverish kiss, never having opened my eyes. His tongue demanded entrance, and I eagerly opened for him. In that moment, there was nothing I wanted more than Jackson over me...on top of me...completing me.

He drank from the well of my mouth, biting into my bottom lip. His hand tugged at the top of my dress, pulling it down so he could cup one of my breasts. I arched, pressing the heavy flesh into his strong palm, relishing the tingles that spread through my chest. I tasted his minty breath as he moaned his pleasure into my mouth. He fondled my breast teasingly. Relief splashed against my senses when he brought the cup of my bra down and grazed his thumb over my aching tip.

"Yes," spilled out of my throat, as if it was ripped directly from the heavens. My cry was guttural and raw. I just needed more, more, more. He swallowed my cry like he needed to breathe it, all lips, teeth, and tongue.

With his thumb and finger, he pulled and pinched the tight peak until the pain somehow became pleasure in my core. I gripped him hard, pulling him to me, finally scratching my nails down the skin on his back like I'd daydreamed about doing earlier. He slid my bra all the way down just then, exposing my chest fully so that he could grope both breasts greedily, tugging and sucking at each tip, driving me insane with lust.

"So fucking perfect," he purred.

Sparks flew as the wet heat of his tongue sent ribbons of pleasure down to the ache between my legs. Heat infused my stomach, and I pressed against his erection, relishing the heavy growl that left his lips.

I didn't know how it was possible with how much pain medicine I was on, but it felt like I could come just by the attention he was currently giving my breasts. I scooted closer to him so that my center was directly against his raging hard on. He slid his hands along my ass and gripped me firmly, moving himself against my clit, sending sparks all over my body.

He slipped one hand into my underwear and plunged two fingers into me.

I cried out, ecstasy invading every facet of my being. His long fingers pressed high and deep, sending waves of pleasure rippling through me as he hit just the perfect spot. He pumped his fingers in and out of me, driving me wild. He circled just the outside of my clit, never going to the place I wanted him most.

While he moved in and out of me, he moved his other hand up to hold my neck possessively, and when he did so, his thumb passed over a sensitive part of my head where I'd hit it.

I gasped as pain flooded me, drowning my lust like a bucket of ice water.

"Shit! Fuck. I'm so sorry."

Jackson scrambled out of bed and stalked to the other side of the room, pulling at his hair. "I can't control myself around you," he growled. "We can't do that while you're recovering from a fucking concussion." He gestured to my body like it should be obvious. "We're not touching if I get back in that bed."

I didn't mention that it wasn't my idea for me to be here or in his bed in the first place.

And I definitely wasn't the one to kiss him.

He walked towards me cautiously and slid into bed like he was scared I was going to jump him.

As he laid down, he took a deep breath. His chest went up and down, and I couldn't take my eyes off the hills and valleys of his perfectly sculpted frame. He somehow looked even more defined than he'd been the last time I'd seen him. I wanted to rub my hands all over that perfect skin again, just to see how he would respond. He stared up at the ceiling, contemplative and brooding.

I kept my hands to myself and just watched him, waiting to hear what he was thinking so hard about.

"I don't know what I'm doing," he muttered to himself.

I traced his features with my gaze, memorizing everything just in case this was the last time I ever got this close to him again. His hair looked more silver than gold in the moonlight, casting him more as the dark, mournful prince than the golden king he was by the light of day.

He turned to me all of a sudden. "Why were you so scared tonight?" he demanded.

"What do you mean?"

"Why was Caiden the first person you thought would push you down the stairs? Why were you so scared?"

I gaped at him, my mouth opening and closing, no words coming out. Not once in all these years had he ever come even close to asking me for my version of what happened. Not once had he ever asked me about Caiden.

"Did you feel like he would do something to get back at you because of that summer? Because Caiden's not like that. He was asking about you as soon as he could. He misses the hell out of you."

That feeling that had begun to wind its way through my veins, the one that felt suspiciously like hope...it evaporated in an instant, leaving nothing but ash and disappointment.

We looked at each other for a moment, and I registered the confusion in his gaze as he saw what must look like utter devastation in mine.

I fixed my clothes and then turned over so I could get away from that stare of his.

He didn't say another word.

Despite what had just happened, the pain medicine and how heavy my head felt made it easy to fall back asleep.

The next time I woke up, it was to heat, a veritable inferno that covered every one of my limbs. Jackson surrounded me, his large legs and arms enclosing me tightly. I didn't know how it was possible for me to feel so sheltered, so secure...even after everything...but I did.

"You didn't think he would push you to get back at you, did you? You were just scared," he said hollowly, and somehow, I knew that he hadn't slept at all. I stiffened, and he pulled me against him so that I was lying against his chest, his steady heartbeat keeping me grounded in the moment.

"Because I've been thinking about it, going over the night of the accident and tonight over and over again these last few hours...and I can't get that look you had out of my head. It was like you'd experienced evil. You were scared down to your soul." He idly traced down my spine.

He sat us up abruptly, making me look at him as he held my face with both hands. "What haven't you told me?" His tone was harsh and demanding. And it pissed me off.

How. Dare. He.

How dare he demand answers when he wouldn't let me have even one answer all those years ago? How dare he demand answers when I had to recover from my injuries all alone? Memories of how excruciating PT was, how I had to relearn how to walk...how painful my surgeries were barreled through my mind. My head hurt so fucking bad right now, and once again, it was the Jackson show. It was all about what *he* wanted.

This night was giving me whiplash with how soft he was in the beginning. But this...this was the Jackson I knew.

I tried to lash out and slap his face, but the pain of moving was too much. Jackson was holding me in place anyway. He pulled me back against his chest, and it was a testament to how in pain I was that I didn't even bother struggling.

His body was shaking as he held me tighter, as if he was having an internal debate.

This time, I didn't fall back asleep.

By the time daylight cracked through the window, I felt even more like shit than I had the night before. And Jackson didn't look any better. He had held me the rest of the night, not letting me move an inch. The intensity of his thoughts barreled against me. It was like he was trying to see inside my head and uncover my secrets.

Strangely, the urge to blurt everything out wasn't there. There had been a time for Jackson to believe me.

And it had passed.

In the light of day, it was easy to remember why I'd said goodbye in the library stacks. Because there had been a time for Jackson to be my hero. And he had failed, a million times over.

I didn't think it was possible for him to make that up to me.

"I need to get back," I told him hoarsely when he still hadn't let go, and I could tell by the light that was coming in from the window that it was getting later and later in the day. I didn't have any intention of going to class, but I at least could get a little bit of sleep while Melanie was in class.

"Fine," he said stiffly as he got out of bed. I carefully averted my eyes from his too beautiful form as he disappeared into the bathroom.

I grabbed my crutches that Jackson had brought in while I was asleep, and hobbled into the hallway, looking for another bathroom, found one, and then promptly gasped when I saw myself in the mirror. My eyes looked like a raccoon's, and my hair looked like squirrels had taken up residence in it.

I can't believe Jackson actually kissed me looking like this...

I felt around the back of my head and neck to see how it was faring, and winced when I happened upon a particularly sensitive area.

I felt pretty pathetic in that moment. The woman staring back at me in the mirror looked haunted, exhausted...hopeless.

Is this how it would be forever?

My thoughts drifted to that feeling of terror as I'd begun to fall down the stairs. In the light of day, it didn't seem as clear that someone had pushed me on purpose as it had last night. Was I just being paranoid? The house had been crowded after all.

And what did it mean for me if it had been on purpose? Who was targeting me?

"Everly?!" Jackson's voice sounded down the hallway. It was a little panicked.

I took a deep breath and crutched my way out of the bathroom. "I'm right here," I called out, and he appeared around the corner, looking relieved to see me.

"You shouldn't have gotten up without me," he scolded

me. I just rolled my eyes. I'd had to do a lot of hard things without him. This was easy compared to those things.

Jackson helped me back down the hallway, and I actually paid attention to his place this time. Everything was decorated in muted greys and blacks. It was austere... perfectly neat. Everything looked like it had been placed there on purpose.

It looked more like a museum than a home. Although saying that...what did I know about a home?

"Nice place," I commented as he opened the garage door for us to leave.

"Yeah," he grunted, evidently back to responding to me in monosyllables, even after what we'd shared last night.

He helped me into his truck, and then we were off, heading back to campus.

We went through a coffee shop drive-through, and before I could give him my order, he told the barista my exact drink.

It was so bad how happy it made me that he still remembered that detail. So bad.

The barista handed him our drinks, and he gave me mine nonchalantly, as if I wasn't having a freak-out in the passenger seat next to him.

We continued to drive quietly.

"Do you still journal?" he suddenly asked.

It was a really random thing for him to say. "Um yeah, every day, just like always," I responded quietly, thinking about the spot under my bed where I'd moved them to after keeping them in my car for the first part of the semester.

He nodded, evidently not having anything for follow-up.

We pulled to the front of my dorm, and he shut off the truck and proceeded to open his door.

"What are you doing?" I asked, panicking for some reason.

"Helping you inside of course."

"I don't need your help," I spat at him, irrationally angry, even as I hung on to the coffee he'd just purchased for me so perfectly.

"Why are you fighting me so hard?" he snarled, turning towards me.

I gaped at him. "What part of 'we're done' did you not hear?"

"We're never going to be done. It doesn't matter what you say. You're poison, but even if I have to die to taste you, that's what I'll do."

I laughed bitterly, even as his words did something crazy to my insides.

"And what about your brother?" I goaded him.

"What about my brother, are you going to start sleeping with him again?"

My face paled as we just stared at each other. The words hovering in the air between us, highlighting the damage and broken shards that was our relationship in glowing letters that couldn't be ignored.

"Fuck," he muttered, pulling at his hair. I took a deep, quivering breath and then opened the truck door, practically falling out as I tried to balance my crutches and my coffee.

He got out of the truck and hurried after me as I clumsily made my way up the dorm steps, inside, and up to my room.

I was sweating by the time we got up there, my head throbbing like someone had taken drum sticks to it.

My hands shook as I tried to unlock my door. Letting out a growl of frustration, Jackson grabbed the keys from my hand and quickly unlocked the door to reveal a blissfully Melanie-free room.

"You can go now," I muttered as I made my way to the bathroom so that I didn't have to look at him. I thought I heard rustling and the sound of drawers opening through the door as I went to the bathroom and washed my hands, but when I got out, Jackson was sitting on my bed.

"Why are you still here?"

"Just get in your bed, and then I'll leave," he responded calmly, rolling his eyes.

I looked around the room suspiciously, trying to see if anything looked out of place...but everything looked normal. Melanie's half of the room looked like a bomb had gone off, per usual, and her things were bleeding into my perfectly organized side of the room...also per usual.

Just wanting him to leave, I crutched over to the bed and almost let out a sob of relief at how good it felt to lay down. All my aches from falling down the stairs were seeping into my muscles beyond the more noteworthy injuries that already hurt.

Add in the sleepless, emotion-filled night I'd had, and I was ready to sleep for forever.

I turned my back towards him, ignoring how good it felt for him to brush his lips across my cheek before he quietly left the room, shutting the door behind him.

What did it mean that I felt lonelier than ever the second I couldn't hear his footsteps?

There was nothing I could do to fix what had broken between myself and Jackson Parker.

Then why the hell was my heart saying otherwise?

9

Jackson

Her journals burned my skin as I smuggled them out of her room. The idea had come to me last night. Everly had been a dedicated journaler since she was a little girl. Evidently, a therapist had suggested it after the whole thing with her father blowing his brains out, and she'd kept it up.

If she wasn't going to tell me what happened that summer, I was going to find out myself. I barreled down the stairs, half-expecting her to come out of her room, screeching for me to come back at any moment.

But thankfully, I was able to make it out of the dorm building, Everly-free.

I drove like a madman back to my place, not even thinking for a moment about attending classes when I had years' worth of her journals to go through.

Maybe I should have felt some kind of guilt for what I was about to do, but Everly James was a mystery that I had to solve, in any way possible.

And like I'd said from the beginning, I'd long ago stopped feeling guilt for my out of control reactions when it came to her.

I turned the corner to get on my street, and I let out a low curse when I saw Caiden's silver Range Rover parked in my driveway. He was leaning against it, typing on his phone. The car had been a "thank you for being alive" present from the parents, and Caiden was all about it.

I nodded at him as I opened the garage and pulled in. He was waiting for me by the garage door when I got out.

"I didn't expect to see you here," I told him. For some reason I didn't want to identify, I left the journals in my truck, not wanting Caiden to see them and ask about them. I was sure he would've recognized Everly's writing right away.

"Just wanted to see if you've heard how Everly was after last night. You never answered my texts," he said casually as he followed me into my townhome.

This was my brother, the person I'd shared a womb with...yet the concept of him sharing my space right now was making me itchy and uncomfortable.

"I just dropped her off at her dorm actually. She came over last night so that I could watch after her."

Caiden abruptly stopped following me and cleared his throat. I opened the refrigerator, not wanting to see his reaction to what I'd just said.

And because just the thought of last night made me hard. Those lips...the sounds she made when she was right on the cusp of coming...

Who needed porn when they had Everly James?

"I thought you guys weren't exactly getting along," he said. I could tell he was trying to sound like he was disinterested, but I knew Caiden. He was hanging on the edge of his seat...metaphorically speaking.

"I wanted to make sure that she was all right. The only other option she had was that blue and pink haired chick's dorm room floor. Didn't sound comfortable after you were pushed down the stairs."

"Pushed down the stairs? She said she was pushed?"

I finally picked a soda from the fridge and turned around to study my twin.

It was amazing really...how fast one could recover from a years-long coma. Caiden looked like the epitome of health. He had been working hard to get ready for next year's football season, and I had a suspicion he was already getting lucky with the ladies.

What if he's gotten lucky with Everly?

The words twisted inside of me, weaving their way insidiously through my brain, even though I knew the idea was next to impossible. I was always watching Everly, couldn't keep my eyes off her. I would have known if Caiden had moved in.

Right?

Just like I'd known back then?

"Yep, she's had some really weird things happen to her since starting at the academy," I told him. I'd only played a part in the snake incident. It was supposed to be a "get the fuck out of here" prank, since I knew she was terrified of snakes, but she'd held on.

The other stuff though...the stuff that I'd dragged from Lane once I'd heard whisperings of it from the football team...that was someone else. And I wasn't happy about it.

And now someone had pushed her.

"Did anything happen when she was over here?" Caiden asked, studying me just as hard back as I was studying him. I reared back at the question, since I felt like it seemed a little odd that he had moved on from the fact that Everly had been intentionally pushed down a flight of stairs so quickly.

Did anything happen...

"Because I really don't think either of us should go there again," he continued, still staring at me.

My heart dropped.

He pushed his hair out of his face. I still wasn't used to how long he wore it now. "I loved her, man. I fucking loved her more than anything. I think it would *kill* me if something started up between you guys now, after everything that's happened. I'm trying to move on. But it's hard, ya know? She won't even talk to me. She won't give me any kind of fucking closure. It's like I don't exist."

Her face as she looked at him with terror last night flashed through my mind. My stomach was in knots as guilt threatened to eat all of my internal organs while I listened to what my twin brother was saying.

How was I supposed to tell him that giving up Everly wasn't an option for me anymore? That despite what she'd done, she was inside of me? A vital part of me just like my lungs or my heart. Except there wasn't a surgery that could get her out. She couldn't be transplanted.

Fuck...was he crying?

"Caid..." My words drifted off. What could I say? I was a terrible person, the worst in fact.

"Let's both skip and hang out today. I have the new Madden game," I told him, clapping him on the shoulder before he did something terrible like make me promise not to get close to Everly. I didn't want to have to lie outright.

I was hoping the journals would help kill whatever had taken root inside of me.

"Sounds good," he told me as he took a deep breath, shooting me that trademark Caiden grin.

We headed into my living room, where I turned on my Playstation and away we went.

Hours passed, and for once, it was like nothing had happened. We played videogames, ordered pizza, even had a few of our teammates over to hang out.

And I didn't think once about those journals.

EVERLY

I had been tempted to skip classes again, but creative writing was today and it was my favorite.

Professor Brady was the best professor at this school. I would fight anyone about it. The passion he had for his subject and his students...it couldn't be matched. I'd become ten times the writer I'd been when I started the class because of him.

It also helped that he was really nice to look at.

Really nice.

It was also thankfully Jackson-free now because of him not wanting intense classes while he was helping Caiden recover...or at least that's what I'd heard his reason was for dropping the class.

Professor Brady looked up in alarm when I walked through the classroom door, right at the bell, hobbling in on my crutches.

"Everly, what happened?" he exclaimed as my cheeks flushed from the fact that everyone in the classroom was watching me.

"A tumble down some stairs," I told him, of course leaving out the fact that I'd tumbled because I'd been pushed.

The professor took a step forward, as if he was going to

try and help me, and I maneuvered as fast as I could to my seat, not wanting to cause a scene.

Professor Brady looked at me with a frown before he began to talk about this week's writing prompt. As usual, I was able to immerse myself in his words and began writing as soon as he gave us the okay.

The class passed by in a flash.

"Everly, can you stay after for a moment?" Professor Brady asked right after the bell had rung to signal the end of class.

I nodded, frowning as the rest of the class left the room, some of them giving me furtive glances that I didn't want to try and understand.

"What's up, Professor?" I asked after I finagled myself and my crutches through the desks and up to his desk at the front of the room.

"I wanted to talk about the story you did last week, but I also wanted to make sure you were okay." Professor Brady's hazel eyes bore into me, and I shifted uncomfortably under his stare.

"I'm fine. I have a concussion and a bruised leg...but it could have been a lot worse."

"You know you can let me know if you ever need help," he said, leaning towards me. I had always been the most comfortable around Professor Brady, even considering him a friend. That's why it was weird the strange prickles going down my spine at the way he was looking at me.

There was just...more in his gaze than usual.

But I had to be imagining that, right? I had hit my head pretty hard just a day ago.

But then he leaned towards me and pushed a piece of hair behind my ear. My breath froze in my body. No, no, no. What was he doing?

Heartbreak Lover

Couldn't I just have one thing in my life that was okay?

I took a step back, and his face fell a bit in disappointment, like he'd been expecting me to jump into his embrace with his touch.

"What about my paper did you want to talk about?" I asked, keeping my voice neutral.

He pushed my paper across his desk towards me, a bright red A gleaming at the top of it. As I reached out to grab it, his hand covered mine, lightly stroking the skin.

"I'd like to talk about the progress you've made this semester, preferably at dinner?"

I opened my mouth and then closed it. My words had been failing me the last few days.

"Everly—" Jackson's voice echoed through the doorway, making Professor Brady and I both jump. I pulled my hand out from under the professor's, my cheeks burning as if Jackson had just caught me doing something wrong.

"Mr. Parker, are you here to talk to me?" Professor Brady asked calmly, like Jackson hadn't just walked in on him propositioning a student.

"Just coming to pick up Everly," Jackson answered coldly, intense dislike written all over his face.

"I didn't know you were friends with Ms. James."

"Hmm, that's interesting."

I grabbed my paper and my backpack, and crutched over to the doorway where Jackson was waiting.

"Think about what I said," Professor Brady said sinfully behind me.

I waved at him over my shoulder, unable to turn around and face him after what had just happened.

Why me?

Jackson waited until we had turned the corner, and then he pushed me into an empty classroom.

"Moving onto professors, Everly?" he asked mockingly as he pushed me against the wall, leaning against me until I had nowhere to go. His voice was dark and threatening... threaded with danger.

"I-It wasn't what it looked like," I stammered, glaring at the audacity of him daring to accuse me of something...once again.

"You belong to me. How do I get that through your pretty little head?"

I opened my mouth to object that I most certainly did not belong to him, and then he crushed his lips against mine. I opened my mouth to allow him access, and he plundered my mouth fiercely with deep swipes of his tongue. We were all lips, teeth, and tongue, arms desperately pulling at one another like a dam had broken and we couldn't be controlled.

His left hand trailed down my skirt in the back. He slipped under the fabric of my thong and gripped me from behind as he ground himself against me. When he slipped a finger into me, I cried out. His mouth quickly swallowed the sound of my desire.

We were suddenly both fumbling with each other's clothes, and I found myself sliding my hand into his briefs and stroking his length, obviously having lost my mind.

"Just like that," he breathed against my lips, his gaze hooded and lust-ridden.

Jackson trailed his lips down my neck while he hiked my skirt up and pulled my underwear to the side.

"Mine," he whispered against my skin as he bit down on my shoulder. My chest was heaving as I watched the feral gleam in his eyes.

He picked me up just then, his arms under my legs and ass as he spread my legs wide. Suddenly, he was on his knees, my legs supported by his shoulders, and he licked me, dipping his tongue inside me. It was too much, yet not enough. I struggled to close my legs, the sensations coming from his ministrations bordering on that line between pain and pleasure. His strong hands prevented me from closing them.

I gripped his hair as he swirled his tongue along my clit.

"So fucking perfect," he breathed against my sensitive skin, the sound of his voice sending me spiraling towards the cliff I was desperate to jump off.

He lapped at me like I was his favorite dessert, and then he pressed down hard, sucking with all his might and sending me shattering into a million pieces.

I convulsed against the wall, but before I could recover, he stood up, releasing his length from his briefs. One second passed before he impaled me with one quick thrust, stretching me wide as he started to hammer into me, the room echoing the sound of our hips slapping against each other and our shared moans.

His lips met mine again, and I could taste myself on him, eliciting a whimper that I should be embarrassed of... It sounded so needy.

His eyes held mine, they were dark with possession and want...for me.

He continued to slam in and out of me feverishly. My pleasure built with every stroke, and I lifted my hips to meet his thrusts. I closed my eyes, and a sharp "Look at me," sounded throughout the room.

"This is so good. We're so good. I'm never going to get enough. You're mine. You're mine," he chanted, never taking his sapphire eyes off of me.

This was more than a quick fuck, I realized. This was more.

I didn't want it to be more.

He shifted, changing the angle of penetration, and that was all it took. I split open, screaming out loud as my entire body splintered and fell in a burst of pleasure.

There was only him.

There was only us.

He continued to move against me, and spirals of light started to build in me once again. His perfect thrusts sent me shooting off into the stars, and this time, he followed me, his jaw setting, his teeth clenching down as he let out what almost resembled a roar.

I felt his heat touch my insides, and then he stilled, leaning his weight against me, his chest rising and falling rapidly...the sound of his out of control breaths reverberating in my ears.

It didn't take long for the guilt to hit. And then the disgust quickly followed.

Especially when he pulled out and I actually felt empty, like I needed him inside of me to feel whole.

He tucked himself back into his pants and then set me down, his hand floating up to gently caress my face.

I turned my head away from him, unable to look at him, to see the disgust echoed in his gaze that I'm sure was all over mine.

With shaking hands, I grabbed a pack of wipes I kept in my backpack. Before I could use the wipe, Jackson grabbed it and gently cleaned me.

"I'd rather you not clean up. I'd rather you smelled like me all day."

The door to the classroom opened just then, and a wide-eyed girl that was in my English literature class about fell over when she saw us. Jackson's hand was still up my skirt.

"Sssorry," she said as she scrambled away, the door slamming closed behind her.

"I've got to go to class, Jackson," I told him, pushing his hands away as I grabbed my backpack and my crutches, stumbling all over the place as I did so.

"Everly, we need to talk—"

"We don't need to talk. How I end up having sex with you in a restaurant bathroom, the library stacks...against the wall of a freaking classroom...that says so much about how we don't need to talk. We just need to stay away from each other. I don't know what the fuck I'm doing. Every word you give me is a pretty lie followed with an insult. Fuck," I said again as I made my way out of the classroom, struggling with the heavy door as I did so.

I went to the rest of my classes somehow.

And I'm pretty sure I smelled like him for the rest of the day.

Just like he'd wanted.

10

Jackson

"A classroom, huh?" Caiden asked as I walked into my living room.

"What the fuck?" I snarled, jumping in my boots because my brother was sitting in the dark in my fucking living room.

I was going to have to get his key back if this was what I could expect.

Caiden stood up and stalked towards me, a crazy glimmer in his eyes. "A classroom, huh? Had to do it so the whole campus would find out and know she belonged to you. Jackson always has to get his way. He can't ever leave anything for the rest of us mere mortals." He stood toe to toe with me, and for a second, I worried I would have to fight my brother.

"You promised, Jackson," he hissed.

Anger drowned out the rational part of my brain. "I didn't fucking promise anything, Caiden. You've been asleep for two fucking years, a lot changed before you woke up."

"I was asleep because that girl destroyed me," he roared.

He stalked towards the front door and threw it open as I ran after him.

"And now it seems you want to destroy me too. Thanks, brother," he spat before slamming the door with a loud bang.

I groaned as I leaned my forehead against the door and listened to the sound of him speeding off. All I could hope was that he wouldn't get into a car accident on the way home.

I slid down the door until I was sitting, leaning against it.

Fuck.

I could smell her all over my clothes.

I could still taste her.

She was everywhere, infecting me until I'd lost the ability for rational thought.

She was everything. And she should be nothing.

What the fuck was I doing?

And then I remembered the journals.

Maybe they would hold the key to carving out the piece of me that Everly owned.

Fuck, I hoped so.

Everly

My journals. They were gone. I'd come back to my room to write down the clusterfuck that had taken place today as a way to calm myself.

And they weren't anywhere. I'd made a mess of my side of the room looking for them, and then I'd started going through Melanie's stuff to see if the bitch had hidden them as a joke.

Obviously, it wasn't the best thing to keep freaking journals in your room when you had a psychotic roommate... but I didn't exactly have a home to stash them in.

I needed to find her. I would get the truth out one way or another. I opened my door, prepared to fly off in a rage and comb the whole campus even on my crutches.

And there she was.

Talking to Caiden.

Right outside our room.

Caiden's gaze flicked to me, and he didn't look surprised to see me. Like he knew where I slept all along and he'd just been biding his time to see me.

And what was he doing with Melanie of all people?

Her attention was fixed on him, and she was salivating like he was the most delicious thing she'd ever seen and all she could contemplate in life was how best to eat him.

I wasn't kidding. She really looked like that.

The sound of the door closing behind me caught her attention, and Melanie glared at me.

"What are you doing here?"

"Um, is that a real question? I live here," I told her, trying to keep my gaze averted from Caiden.

"Hey, Everly," he said quietly. My eyes closed unbidden as I remembered when that voice used to be one that I loved the most.

And then the memory of that voice screaming at me in the car that night quickly dispelled any good feelings I might have had in my moment of weakness.

"Caiden," I responded stiffly. "I need to talk to you," I told Melanie.

"Well, I'm busy."

"Did you take my journals?" I asked, shifting uncomfortably under Caiden's gaze. He was well acquainted with my affinity for journaling, as I had spent hours in his room writing while he was doing homework.

Melanie's gaze glimmered maliciously. "Journals? How cute. But no, I have no interest in whatever inane ideas you have going on in your head."

I searched her face for any signs of deceit. There was the usual hate and annoyance, but nothing that signaled that she was lying to me. And I could usually tell.

But if she hadn't taken them, then who had?

I stepped backwards to return to the room, but my curiosity over how Melanie and Caiden knew each other had me acting stupid.

"So…how do you know each other?" I asked quietly.

Something glimmered in Caiden's gaze, as if my question had given him pleasure.

"We just met," Melanie responded quickly.

Lie. She'd just lied to me. She always smoothed her hair behind her left ear when she lied. I'd learned that months ago.

But why would she lie about that? What did it matter if she'd known Caiden for longer than a day?

And why would she care if I knew?

"Cool," I said shortly, backing away quickly to go back into the room.

"Have fun today in class?" Caiden's voice floated after me.

I froze. He couldn't know…could he?

"It was fine," I told him tightly, not turning around to look at him. I disappeared into my room and closed the door as fast as I could, Melanie's cruel laughter echoing around me.

My head hurt from constantly being on guard at this fucking school.

My phone rang just then. It was Landry. I sighed, not knowing what to do. I'm sure that girl had spread it all over campus, if Caiden and Melanie both knew what had happened with Jackson today. Despite what Lane had said about Landry knowing what was going on, I couldn't help but feel guilty.

"Hello?" I answered, trying to keep my voice light and guilt free.

"Hi, sweetheart." Well, that was good. He didn't sound mad. Maybe he didn't know. Although maybe I wanted him to know so I didn't have to tell him myself what happened. "How are you feeling?"

"Crutches were great today, but the swelling's gone down a lot."

"That's good," he said faintly, as if he wasn't really paying attention.

Awkward silence ensued.

"I still can't believe that happened at the party. The team's been questioning everyone. We haven't talked to anyone who saw you fall."

"Yeah, it seemed like people were pretty occupied up on that floor."

More awkward silence.

"So, I heard something today..."

Ahh, here it was.

"Something about you and Jackson...and a classroom."

"Landry," I said softly, feeling so terrible that I just couldn't find it in myself to pick him over Jackson every time it came up.

"Just let me talk," he ordered, his voice speeding up. "Obviously, it fucking sucks to hear something like that. I mean you and I have only kissed. I thought we were finally going somewhere..."

I prepared for the goodbye, stiffening my shoulders, even though he couldn't see me.

"But obviously, I'm doing something wrong. I just need to try harder. Hockey's over now, and I'll be able to give you the attention you deserve."

I had no idea what to say. I had fucked another guy against a wall in a classroom, and he still wanted to date me? What the hell?

"Jackson and I..." I began, needing to explain that I didn't know what was going on with me and him, that I didn't know when...if ever...I would be able to finally say goodbye to Jackson, even when I knew he was doing nothing but ruining my soul.

"I couldn't compete before, because I didn't know it was a competition. But I know Jackson. He's an asshole to his very core. He'll mess up, and I won't. You'll see."

"Oh, Landry."

"Anyways, breakfast tomorrow?" he hurried on before I could say anything. "I'll meet you at your dorm so I can help you carry your bag."

"Sounds good," I said softly, and then he was gone and I was beating myself on the head with my phone, wondering what was broken inside of me that I couldn't just get myself to fall for a guy like Landry.

Of course, it was at that moment that my phone beeped, signaling an incoming text.

It was Jackson.

Jackson: I need to talk to you. Now. It's important.
Me: Where?
Jackson: My place. Please.

What was that I'd just been telling myself? I hesitated, thinking that maybe this was the moment I could take a stand. This was the moment I could say goodbye to Jackson Parker.

But the way he'd said "please." He never said please.

Just this last time, I promised myself.

I didn't know why I bothered to lie to myself anymore.

11

Jackson

It was all I could do to hold on. This time, I could feel myself turning black. I could feel the darkness threatening like a storm on the horizon.

I'd read every word. I'd read every ugly, awful word. Words that destroyed me. Words that changed the fabric of my soul, twisting it and shaping it into something that it should have been all along.

Hers.

I'd made myself start from the beginning. I'd read about how abusive her mother had been, how much we'd failed her by letting her hide it all from us when the signs should have been obvious to us. I'd read about how she both missed and hated her father, how some weeks, her mother had forgotten to get any food for the house. How sometimes, she hadn't had electricity or running water, because her mother had spent all their money on booze and spa treatments she couldn't afford and didn't need. How hungry and alone Everly had felt. Constantly.

And then I'd read about Everly's love story with my brother and I.

And it was a love story, just not the kind that Caiden had wanted.

I could feel the worship and veneration about the two of us, how she felt like we'd saved her.

Not realizing that she was the one who'd saved us.

Or at least, saved me.

It was obvious now, reading it after everything had happened, the way that Caiden had manipulated her... manipulated me.

Starting from when he stole her first kiss by lying about my first kiss.

I still remembered that day, about how she'd approached me with tears in her eyes. How I'd tried to tell her what happened, that Marcy had kissed me...I hadn't kissed her. My pre-teen brain hadn't understood why she was making such a big deal about something that had meant nothing to me.

But now I understood that Caiden, even at thirteen, had been doing everything he could to make sure that "our girl" was only his girl.

And then I got to that summer. The rage simmered inside of me, her words stoking the flames until they burned out of control.

Had Caiden wanted me to lose control that day in that fight at school?

I remembered that night when I'd come home, and how he'd told me that I almost hit Everly during the fight and that I was too dangerous to be around her.

I'd lied to her that next day. Destroying my angel with cruel words in an effort to save her. From me.

When the person she needed saving from was him.

I read his words to her, how he tore her apart all summer, how he controlled her every move. How she longed for me every second of every day.

Just like I'd longed for her.

By the time I got to that night, the one that changed everything, I could barely control myself.

Her words pushed me over the edge.

I read in disbelief how she'd finally gotten the courage to break it off, the guilt she'd felt. I read about me taking her virginity, something I'd so vilely thrown in her face.

I read about the text from Caiden.

And then I read about everything after that. Including that she thought I'd called her and had tried to scream into her phone for help.

It hadn't been me.

My twin brother was the devil. And he'd destroyed my sweet, beautiful, perfect Everly. And I'd helped him.

It was like I was the one on the receiving end of every hit from his fist as I read her words.

I wanted to stop right there. I knew if I looked in the mirror, I'd see the black taking over the blue, but I knew that I had to read to the end.

And I did. I read about how alone she was, every fucking day, when she tried to recover from the injuries that Caiden had made to her body. And the injuries that I had made to her soul.

Long after I'd finished her last words, I sat there, thinking about all the time I'd wasted mourning Caiden and hating Everly.

Caiden should have died in that hospital bed.

The words came sharp and fast, and yet I knew that I meant them down to the marrow of my bones.

My brother had spent years of his life, a wolf in sheep's clothing.

The truth had been right there in front of me this entire time.

I might as well have been the one in that car with her, for all the damage I'd done.

The way she'd described what I said to her in that hospital room, when she'd just woken up and she'd been all alone, her body and life destroyed.

I screamed, the sound of my pain echoing through the room. I picked up my coffee table and flipped it over, the glass vase that my mother had decorated it with crashing to the ground and shattering everywhere.

The bookshelf was next, and then the TV. I destroyed everything in the living room before moving on to the kitchen.

And after I'd destroyed that room, I grabbed a butcher knife from off the counter and held it to my chest, thinking of how good it would feel to slice through the skin and bones and end everything right now.

I didn't deserve to live.

Caiden didn't deserve to live.

The thought had me throwing the butcher knife to the ground with shaking hands.

I sank to my knees and started to weep.

And then there she was, sinking to her knees in front of me.

"It was all Caiden, wasn't it?" I choked out. "He did everything. He hurt you that night."

She stared at me, her beautiful green eyes watery and unfathomable. The truth was there in their depths. The confirmation that every word she'd written was true.

The confirmation that I didn't deserve to breathe the same air as her.

There wasn't a difference between a broken heart and being in a prison, I decided.

The darkness took over after that. And I hoped it would keep me forever this time.

ஃ

Everly

He didn't answer when I knocked.

I huffed as I crossed my arms and looked through the windows, trying to see if I could find any sign of life.

There was no movement through the side windows, but on a closer look...everything looked...destroyed.

I knocked on the door again frantically, thinking Jackson had texted me because his house had been robbed. When he didn't answer again, I tried the doorknob, and the door opened up quietly.

The house was completely still. But you could feel the violence in the air, feel how it had sunk into the walls of the house, and this place would somehow never feel the same.

I walked through the front foyer hesitantly, finally thinking about the fact that if he had been robbed...the robber could still be here. What if Jackson had texted me for help and I was supposed to have called the police?

I shook my head at the ridiculousness of my thoughts. Jackson would obviously have called the police first before "texting" the cripple he fucked on occasion.

I heard movement from the next room, and I continued to walk deeper and deeper into the house, despite the alarms blaring loudly in my head that I needed to retreat and get away from here as soon as possible.

I pulled out my cell phone and dialed Jackson.

I frowned when I heard his phone ringing in the next room.

I went as fast as my bum leg and crutches could take me and then stopped short as I noted the utter destruction of the living room. The foyer had stuff knocked over...but this... There wasn't a single thing in this room that had been left unscathed.

A cry sounded from where I remembered the kitchen was located, and I stumbled towards it, stopping suddenly when I saw the pile of journals that had gone missing from my room.

Jackson had taken them.

He knew.

Looking around the room, I realized that the damage here wasn't from a robbery.

It was from Jackson finding out the truth about the past.

I'd carried the burden of the past for a long time, I knew how heavy it felt.

Jackson was kneeling on the ground, his body racked with sobs. Utter destruction littered the floor around him.

I walked slowly towards him and then knelt in front of him, ignoring the pain in my leg. All I could focus on was his pain and how much it called to me.

He lifted his head and met my gaze, black orbs where blue was usually found.

He'd gone black.

"It was all Caiden, wasn't it?" he asked me in a sorrow ridden voice. "He did everything. He hurt you that night."

I couldn't answer. For so long, I'd dreamed about telling him the truth, and then I'd let that dream go, deciding to let the past lie there because it couldn't be changed, no matter how much I prayed.

And now here it was.

The truth didn't taste as good as I thought it would.

And then Jackson was gone, taken to wherever the darkness called him to.

※

My heart broke all over again those next few days. I couldn't examine how I was feeling about the truth finally being out, because Jackson was falling apart at the seams in a way I'd never seen another person do, not in my entire life. Finding out the truth had broken him.

He alternated between sobbing and screaming those first few hours, self-destructing spectacularly so that his pain was all I could see.

It was the most horrible thing I'd ever seen happen to someone I loved. And I'd seen my daddy blow his brains out on the sidewalk in front of my house.

I'd written all my professors my excuses, telling them my injuries from the fall were too much. And I stayed in that destroyed townhome tending to Jackson. My phone died by the end of the day. I didn't bother charging it.

The days were a blur. Sometime after the first two days, one of his old roommates came by. He'd looked surprised to see me, but he'd taken one look at Jackson's dark eyes and haunted appearance and he'd quickly left, not wanting to deal with Jackson in this state.

I didn't blame him. Jackson had been inconsolable and in an almost constant state of rage. His mind was like a tornado on a rampage, and nothing was safe those first two days.

He slipped into something else entirely after that.

The rage burned off, and something much more sinister

took its place. During that time, I'd never seen someone drink so much in my entire life and remain standing. Though sometimes, he didn't do that either and I had to sleep next to him on either the bathroom floor or the kitchen floor, because he was too heavy to move. Once, we slept on the floor of his shower because he'd passed out in the middle of me washing him. Alcohol was a depressant, this I knew, but he used it like a tranquilizer for his manic behavior, and he gave himself dose after dose until he was out cold. Each morning, I lay with my body wrapped tightly around his and waited. I waited, praying and hoping that would be the morning I'd see blue eyes.

I didn't.

We lay in bed. I'd managed to get him there the night before by stripping myself of all my clothes and offering myself to his demons. I did this because when he wasn't out cold, he was on me. Not in the way he had been those few times.

This was different.

It was rough, needy, crippling, and terrifying. I was a vice, and like the booze, I was soothing. The very fabric of his sanity was stitched into the beat of my heart. Sometimes, he lay for hours with his head on my chest, just listening. I let him. I let him do whatever he needed to survive. I was propped up on my side, leaning over to look down at him. Jackson looked so lost, but he was in there. I knew he was. Cupping his cheek in my hand, I watched as he leaned into it for comfort.

"Jackson. Come back to me."

Leaning down, I rested my forehead against his. His eyes were so haunting, his ghosts flickering amongst the black staring back at me.

"Follow the sound of my voice and come home."

His eyes closed at my words, and a tear slipped out. I kissed him hard, pouring every piece of whatever this was that I felt for him into every swipe of my tongue, graze of my teeth, and movement of my lips.

I was crying by the time our kiss ended. "Come back to me, Jackson." He didn't answer. He rarely did.

After the anger had subsided, he rarely spoke at all. He would whisper my name sometimes when he slept, but that was it. He didn't even say my name when we fucked. It was like this part of him was incapable of connecting with any of the feelings he knew when his eyes were blue.

I hated that for him. My tears fell onto his cheeks, but he didn't hold me. His body lay practically unmoving in my arms, but his eyes never left mine.

I resorted to begging after a while.

"You aren't allowed to be like this. You don't get to feel sorry for yourself, Jackson Parker. You should have believed in me. You should have loved me the way that you'd promised all those years ago," I raged at him.

Nothing. No reaction.

I grabbed his face and kissed him even harder than before, so hard I could taste my tears on his lips. Then I lay on his chest, holding him tighter than I'd held on to anything in my entire life.

I realized once again how in love with Jackson I was. I'd told myself that I wasn't, but the truth was right here, practically streaming out of every one of my pores as I held him tightly.

Love for me had always been dark and ugly, only seen in those shadowed places that no one wanted to speak about.

That's why it was so easy to deny. Because I wanted to believe in the happily ever after, in the prince who charged in on the white horse and saved me.

But I was a fool.

I knew that now.

So, I waited. It took seven days. For seven days, I warded off every nightmare with my heart pressed naked against his. For seven days, I chased away every doubt-induced fever. For seven days, my body was Jackson's salvation when his soul needed safety.

I was fucked raw, emotionally exhausted. Jackson took everything from me. Just like he always had.

Then he opened his eyes.

And I cried when I saw that my favorite shade of blue had once again returned.

But I also cried because despite the fact that Jackson now knew the past, it couldn't change the present. It didn't change the fact that Jackson hadn't been there for me all those years when I needed him the most.

I cried because those eyes of his told me that Jackson Parker loved me.

I cried because it was too late.

12

Jackson

The problem with being bipolar was that when I went into those truly black cycles, I couldn't remember much...if anything when I emerged.

But this one was different.

Because for the first time, I hadn't been alone.

Everly had stayed.

When I came to, I saw my marks on her body, I could recall flashes of using her body over and over again as an outlet for my pain. I remembered her tears as she cried for me, the demon who didn't deserve her grief.

Unlike the other times, where I'd woke up to piles of trash and regrets, my body felt sated and satisfied. Like it had been loved over and over again, brought back to life by her touch.

"Hi," I murmured.

She smiled, but her smile didn't reach her eyes.

If I was thinking that me knowing the truth was going to bring her back to me, I'd been wrong. That much was clear.

She stayed with me for the rest of the day but we didn't talk about it. We didn't mention anything dark or heavy, even though I was bursting to beg her for forgiveness, to beg her to love me again.

She left with a muted goodbye, my thanks echoing after her. I'd used her body for days, yet we didn't even part with a hug, much less a kiss.

She waved goodbye before limping her way out the door. She'd stayed with me for so long that her leg had healed enough that she didn't need crutches anymore.

The sun faded away as I watched Lane pull up to the house. Lane asked Everly something when she opened the door, and she just shook her head. She looked exhausted and pale as she got in.

Like always, I'd taken something from Everly without giving her anything in return. That she wanted that is.

Everly had my entire heart and soul.

But I didn't think there was a piece of her that wanted that.

So I sat there as Lane pulled away. And I was furious at myself, yes. But my anger soon drifted towards the person whose real sins this all was.

The Judas who'd kissed me on the cheek while stabbing me in the back.

My brother, who hadn't even sent one text message in the seven fucking days I'd been out.

My fury towards Caiden built while I sat there, until I no longer could see the sunset. All I could see was his face and how much I wanted to destroy it.

The betrayal was so thick that I could taste it. I had to rethink everything, look back on our whole lives together in a different light, examining everything to see just how far his manipulation had gone.

And I didn't just want revenge because of what he'd done to me, how he'd ripped the love of my life away from me and convinced me to cast her aside like yesterday's used goods.

I wanted revenge for her. There wasn't anything I could do to truly give back to Everly what she'd lost, but I could at least make Caiden pay.

I got into my truck, and I headed towards campus.

I wasn't a violent person. I kept my crazy side locked in tight so that it could only escape when I went black. This was the first time that I was intentionally looking to incite a fight with a perfectly cool head.

I had tunnel vision by the time I parked outside the apartment where he stayed with two others from the team. I knew there would be consequences.

But I couldn't fucking care less.

I ran up the stairs and pounded on the door, adrenaline coursing through me.

Derek, a second-string wide receiver on the team opened the door.

"Oh hey, Jackson," he said, reaching out to give me a high five.

I ignored him and pushed my way into the apartment.

Caiden was in the living room with two others from the team, all of them drinking beers and holding Xbox controllers.

Caiden looked up, and our gazes locked.

"Well, isn't this a pleasant surprise—" he got out before I walked over and grabbed his shirt with two hands, hoisting him off the couch and giving him a hard shake.

I could hear my teammates yelling faintly, but everything else was white noise.

There was only Caiden and I.

"I'll kill you," I murmured right before I let him go and slammed my fist into his face.

"Fuck!" Caiden yelled, holding his nose that I hoped was broken. Blood was trickling down his face.

"What the fuck, Jackson? What is wrong with you?" he yelled.

"I know about everything with Everly, Caiden. I know what a spineless worm you are."

"Everly? I don't know what you're talking about?" he tried to say, but I was on him again, laying my fist into his face again and again.

He roared in pain and then slammed into me.

We fell to the ground. Caiden was able to get a few good punches in before I was able to roll him on his back. My hands enclosed around his neck, squeezing until his eyes started to bulge. He still hadn't regained his full strength from the coma, and he was no match for me.

Caiden suddenly landed a punch to my chin, and it knocked the wind out of me for a moment, giving him enough time that he could roll us again as he tried to return the beating I'd just given him. His face was swollen and bruised, and I savored the sight of it, wishing inanely that Everly was here to see it. I'd read about her injuries. I wasn't sure I could pull off giving Caiden a ruptured spleen, but I'd love to try.

Who cared if my parents disowned me and I went to jail?

I was brought back to the fight when Caiden hit me right in the left eye and my eyebrow split open, sending blood splattering all over my face.

I suddenly rolled again and pinned him down with one hand on his chest. I drew my fist back again and again, punching him. It was cathartic really how good it felt every time my fist connected with his face.

Heartbreak Lover

A pair of arms grabbed me from behind, and I began to struggle, able to level one more hit right at Caiden's throat that had him gasping for breath.

"Jackson, what the fuck. Get ahold of yourself." The yells of my teammates filled the air, and I took a deep breath, trying to control myself from hitting one of them.

The four of them were looking at me like I was a monster. Little did they know the biggest monster they would encounter in their life lay on the ground in front of us. I grinned savagely as I saw that I'd beaten him almost unrecognizable. I'm sure I was a sight. I could taste the coppery blood swirling in my mouth, all over my teeth.

Caiden groaned something unintelligible from his place on the ground.

I kicked him in the stomach, laughing when I heard the sound of his rib cracking. I think that had been one of Everly's injuries as well.

Two of my teammates grabbed me again and forced me back.

Caiden lifted his head up and stared at me, cold fury written all over his features, and his face looked like ground hamburger as he groaned again.

"Man, what the hell is wrong with you?" my left tackle, Freddie, snarled at me, staring at me like I was a stranger.

"That asshole right there likes to abuse girls," I responded, giving him the short version of what was a very long story.

Freddie gaped at me. "Caiden? Dude..."

"I don't remember anything," Caiden mumbled, the words hard to make out.

"That's convenient," I snarled. "You seem to know exactly what I'm talking about though."

"You think I don't know something happened with

Everly? You think I don't see how she looks at me like I'm a demon whose sole purpose is to destroy her life? The last thing I remember, Everly was my best friend, the girl I'd loved since the second I laid eyes on her as a little kid. I'm not an idiot, Jackson. I can connect the dots. I just didn't..."

"You just what? Didn't know that you beat the crap out of her? That she was in the hospital for weeks and then in physical therapy for months after that? That she walks with a limp because of what you did to her? That you lied to me about it so I would hate her? You didn't know any of that?"

It didn't matter to me that he claimed he didn't remember. I saw him now. People didn't change, not like that. Caiden didn't get a brain transplant during his coma.

Caiden held up a beseeching hand. "I'm not saying you aren't right. But I don't remember what happened that night or that summer. I can't comprehend ever doing that to her. She was everything to me. She *still* is everything to me."

"You and me, we're done. We won't ever come back from this. If you see me, walk the other direction." I gave him one last warning glance before I stalked out, my teammates' stunned silence following me.

I couldn't change the past, but I would do whatever I could to get Everly back. And if that didn't work, I'd at least make sure that no one would ever hurt her again.

It would be my life's mission.

And still, it wouldn't be enough to make up for what I did.

Everly

I felt like a stranger in my own skin.

It was a weird floating feeling, like I was wading through water.

I was going through all my normal motions, but it was like I was seeing everything through a fogged lens.

The week where Jackson had used my body over and over again had left me lost.

"The only way to get over someone is to get under someone else," Lane teased me, trying to make me laugh. I'd told her all of my secrets in the car on the way home from Jackson's. They'd burst out of me, just like the tears I couldn't seem to control.

She'd tried for days to make me feel better.

All her efforts did the same thing as they did now.

Nothing.

I couldn't even imagine having sex with anyone else. Ever.

It was like he'd done something to me, burned himself into my skin, so just the thought of someone else made me break out in hives.

"Everly," a voice called from behind me, a voice that I'd heard in every nightmare for the last two years.

I stopped, gripping Lane's arm. She winced from how hard I was holding her and then turned around to see who it was. Her eyes widened. I took a deep breath and turned. And then promptly stumbled in place.

Caiden…looked awful.

I mean, he was almost unrecognizable. His face was swollen, cut, and bruised, a mixture of red, purple, and blue like someone had thrown a macabre set of paints at him.

One of his eyes was completely swollen shut, and I could see a set of handprints around his neck.

I absorbed every detail of Caiden's injuries, and a light flickered on inside of me. I knew who had done this.

Jackson.

And even if he hadn't done this to avenge me or make me feel better...

It did make me feel better. It really did.

Some of the fog that had been hovering around me dissipated right then and there.

And I smiled.

Caiden flinched at the smile, like I'd actually thrown a left hook instead.

He fidgeted in place, his gaze dancing all over my features.

"What happened to you?" Lane blurted out. "Not that you don't deserve it of course."

He ignored her, which was something that Jackson was prone to do as well. It was fucking annoying.

"LyLy."

I flinched at the nickname, wanting to cut my ears off or rip the words from my brain somehow.

"Everly," he amended. "Can I talk to you...alone?" He shot Lane a loaded look.

"We don't have anything to say to one another," I told him resolutely, hate thick in my throat.

"I have a lot to say actually," he responded quietly. "If you would just give me the chance."

"Come on, Lane." I grabbed her arm and began to pull her away, walking as fast as I could. I didn't even know where I was going, I just knew that I had to get away from him.

"Do you think—" Lane began.

"No. There's nothing he could say that I would want to hear." But even as I said the words, I remembered a time when that boy had been everything, when he'd defended me when no one else but Jackson would. I remembered him buying me lunch every day, sticking up for me in front of his parents…I remembered it all.

And a little piece of me weakened, a tiny chunk of the wall of hate I'd built around everything inside of me that was Caiden crumbled to the ground.

But still, I kept walking.

※

IT WAS RAINING OUTSIDE. I used to love the rain. Now I hated it, avoided it like it would burn my skin if a raindrop dared to touch me.

I was alone in my room. Melanie had been scarce over the last few months, I assumed with a new boytoy. It was fabulous.

So here I was, sitting in my desk chair, staring out my window at the rain like some kind of character in an Enya song.

I stood up suddenly, my chair toppling over behind me at the movement.

The truth was, I didn't hate the rain…I was scared of the rain.

And that was just about the dumbest thing I'd ever heard of.

I was going to go out and walk in the rain until I wasn't scared anymore…until I was clean.

Maybe the rain could wash away every trace of that night.

I was willing to try anything at this point.

As I walked down the hall of my dorm, I ignored all the looks that I got. I'd become somewhat of a laboratory animal these last few weeks. Ever since the classroom incident.

Shrugging off their looks was becoming easier and easier. Maybe one of these days, I would finally grow a thick skin.

I hesitated before I took my first step out into the rain. It was falling steadily, not quite a downpour but not a sprinkle either.

The first step nauseated me. The feeling of the raindrops splattering on my skin almost felt like fire licking at me. But as I took one more step, and then another…it got easier, just as all things did the more you did them.

Why hadn't I done this before?

When I was fully submerged under the falling sky, I turned my head up and welcomed the feeling of the rain tumbling on my face.

And maybe I did feel a little cleaner.

Until I heard Caiden's voice once again.

"Everly," he breathed.

Closing my eyes, I slowly turned and faced him.

He stood there, soaking wet, like he'd been waiting for me for hours right in that spot. His hands were in his pockets, his broken face still beautiful, despite what I suspected were Jackson's best attempts to change that.

"What do you want from me, Caiden?"

"I don't remember what I did. I don't have a clue how I'm even capable of doing what Jackson told me I did. I can't even comprehend it. But I'm so fucking sorry for it." His voice broke as he spoke, his tears joining the rain splashing down his face.

"I'll do anything to get you to forgive me. Anything. For almost my whole life, it's been the three of us. And now you're both gone, and I can't even remember why." He pulled at the bottom of his shirt, twisting and turning it like he wanted to rip the fabric in half.

He took a step towards me, and for the first time, I held my ground. My stillness must have given him confidence, because he kept walking until he was right in front of me.

"Please, LyLy, please forgive me. Please know that I won't ever hurt you again. I'll live my life to make you happy. I'll always be here for you. You'll never be alone."

My eyes widened at his words, as they were an echo of words he'd said in our shared past, promises he made to me.

And I knew how those promises ended up.

Broken, just like me.

But I was also so very tired of carrying around all of this hate and fear and disgust for myself, because I still believed whole-heartedly that I carried some of the blame for what happened that summer.

"I forgive you, Caiden," I whispered, the words getting caught in the rain. They sounded wrong as I released them.

His whole face softened. "Thank you," he said, lifting up his hand to touch my face.

I took a step out of reach, and he frowned.

"But we won't ever be the same. We *can't* ever be the same." I sighed, pushing my dripping wet hair from in front of my eyes. "I'll always be grateful to you for everything we had. But we turned into something so ugly that I'll never be able to forget it."

"I'll do anything," he begged, his face the picture of despair, but I held up my hand.

"I'm sorry, but there's nothing you can do. It's just been me these last few years. I've had a lot of time to think." I laughed bitterly. "Did you know I used to visit you? Every week."

His eyes widened.

"I fully own up to my part in what happened. I was weak. I let you and Jackson walk all over me, dictate every part of my life. I was so desperate for you that I didn't listen to the blaring alarms inside of me that told me to run as far away as fast as I could. I would sit by your bedside, and I would tell you over and over again how sorry I was."

A hiccuped sob burst out of my mouth.

"But I've realized now that I didn't need you to forgive me, I needed to forgive myself. And I've done that. And now I've realized that though I don't *want* to live without you, I *can* live without you."

"Everly, please," he begged, dropping to his knees in front of me, mud splashing over his rain-soaked blue jeans.

"Let me go," I breathed, and then I brushed a kiss across his forehead, and I limped away.

The rain really was cleansing after all.

13

I ended up exactly at the place I shouldn't have, soaking wet and shivering.

Jackson stood there in the entryway to his house, a few bruises peppering his otherwise god-like face.

He held out his hand, and even though it felt like I might be repeating the sins of my past, I took it.

I needed the brand of torture that only Jackson could give me.

Jackson walked me to his room.

And everything was different this time.

Different but the same.

Because we'd moved like this together once before...our very first time.

And I'd forgotten how much I loved that, needed that.

The feeling you had when you were making love.

His kiss wasn't hard or demanding like those other times, but it was just as intense, hypnotizing me with its slow, seductive rhythm as one of his hands cradled the back of my head while we stood there by his bed. His touch assaulted me from all angles, a tingling sensation scattering across my skin and shooting between my legs. Grabbing his shirt, I moved against him, letting out a quiet moan as I drove myself crazy.

He enfolded me into his arms, worshipping my mouth with his, my body heating under his touch as he caressed every whispered shadow.

My hands moved everywhere—his shoulders, arms, running over the hard lines of his back. Everything he did taunted the warmth building between my thighs.

Our clothes disappeared, and then without warning, he pushed me to the bed but didn't follow. His breath faltered as he gazed. Slow and deliberate, his inspection was thorough and his voice rough.

"I've never wanted anything more than I want you."

The passionate need in his eyes was replaced with veneration, a worshipping glint as he drank me in.

"Everly," he breathed into the silence, my name a prayer on his lips. Slowly, he laid down with me, bringing a hand up to cup the full weight of my breast. Closing his eyes, he leaned in so his mouth hovered over mine, not touching, just taking.

It felt like he was casting a spell over me, and for once, I didn't want to break it.

He pinched my nipple, pulling until I moaned. The sweet sensation drove through my body, a sharp, inescapable fluttering. He smiled, a slow, beguiling grin as I writhed beneath his dark stare and the attention of his fingers.

"I dream about the way you taste, baby."

My mouth formed a perfect circle, but I said nothing, paralyzed with anticipation. I watched as he dipped down, taking me into his mouth, laving the elongated tip of my breast with his tongue before teasing it between his teeth. I leaned back into the bed, reeling from the pleasure his mouth brought. One at a time, he played with my breasts until I was wet and hungry for him.

"Please," I begged, for what, I didn't quite know. For him to continue, for him to touch me, for him to bring an end to the burning need building between my thighs. Slowly, he moved, his nose trailing along my skin, teasing a path until he pressed into my skin, groaning as he breathed deeply. Eyes trained on mine, he pushed my thighs apart.

"You're intoxicating. Addicting. I'll never get enough." His voice was hot, his breath hotter as he blew against me. Looking up through his lashes, he asked, "Do you want this, baby? Tell me you need this as much as I do."

I was speechless, so he blew against me again. "Say it. I need to hear you."

"Yes." I barely breathed out the word before his head dipped, the tip of his tongue swirling right where I wanted. My body arched off the bed at the sweet carnal sensation, and I moaned loudly. Closing my eyes, I focused on the feeling of him and the tormenting flicks of his tongue.

Wrapping his arms under my hips, he became impassioned, groaning as he lifted me to his mouth. I couldn't move, my only outlet the incoherent words falling almost soundlessly into the still air.

Clenching my hands into the sheets, I surrendered to the beautiful intensity, panting. "Jackson," I cried. His lips closed around my clitoris in response, sucking and rolling it between his teeth. I arched and instinctively moved with him, a wicked, slow dance. The music was his mouth, playing artfully, and all I could do was wait, longing for the crescendo. Releasing my death grip on the sheets, I grabbed the soft silk of his hair as his head swayed between my thighs. He looked up, his blue eyes scorching and erotic, his tongue insistent and hot, teasing but not taking me over the edge.

"Please," I whispered, begging for the push from the burning plateau. His answer was to slide a finger inside my welcoming body. I groaned again. The longing and desire built, the friction of his finger along with his mouth took me higher, faster than I thought possible. I writhed against him, the dance becoming feverish. I needed; I wanted.

"Don't stop."

Two fingers plunged into me once, twice, his tongue flicked and rolled again and again, and he launched me beyond the brink. I exploded, screaming out in awe as the crescendo hit violently. Waves of pleasure crashed through my entire body, and I bowed into him once more. His mouth and fingers continued moving on me, in me, pushing my orgasm on and on. When I couldn't stand it anymore, I tugged his hair, pulling him up to me. Diving into his mouth, I tasted myself on his tongue, relishing the feel of his lips stroking over mine. Without thought, I grabbed his bottom lip between my teeth, sucking on it, mimicking what he just did to me. Drinking in his low moan, I spurred him on for more.

"What do you want, little angel?"

"I want you."

"What do you need?" he taunted again.

"You, it's always you," I cried softly, pulling him to me.

In one swift move, he slid into me, our eyes locked together, and he took in my breath, hovering over my open mouth to take me in again and again. My hips met his in slow motion as I felt every inch of him inside of me, a full tormenting stretch. His name fell so easily from my lips, a whispered shadow in the darkened room. Dipping his head, he took my nipple into his mouth, sucking on it. Not to draw pleasure from pain, as I'd found he was so good at doing, but an easy pull to draw out a sweet pulse that I felt not just in my breast, but between my legs as well. Burying his head in the crook of my shoulder, he traded between his own hushed moans to sharing sweetness in my ear.

"So beautiful... Want you to feel everything... Do you feel that?"

It was beautiful. Everything about this night with him was beautiful. And I did feel every brush of his chest against mine, his warm breath as it rushed my skin, calling each nerve to attention. Each of his heartbeats was intensified, and his pounding pulse had a direct line to mine. It seemed they needed to thrum together. But more than that, I felt the need to keep him next to me, to have more moments like this one. To let him in, give him more of me, maybe even everything, so there was a possibility of a forever made up of him and me.

He placed his hands on either side of my face, cradling me like I was something precious. His breath, his body, we became one, and I began to make love with Jackson Parker —sweet, beautiful, passionate love.

I felt it all. I felt all of him. My hips moved, rounding gently at first, pulling him in and out at a taunting, tortuous pace.

The joy in this moment was almost more than I could bear. It was so fucking, achingly sweet. My thoughts scattered, frayed with unbridled tension, and I dissolved around him, mind and body surrendering to this mystifying connection between us that I was starting to believe was unbreakable.

"So good, little angel. You feel so good wrapped around me," he breathed into my mouth, just before licking and claiming me with a long kiss. His tongue mimicked the rock and sway of his hips, deep, deeper still with each push forward. I took in every sound he made and sucked on his lips, and then the rough bristle of his chin and down his neck, savoring the sweet sheen of sweat that coated his chest, making it slide onto mine.

Straightening his arms, Jackson looked down, into my eyes and then along every line of my chest as it rose and fell beneath him.

I love you, he said, but no sound came with the words. I lived and died with those words, holding them tight inside of me until they became a part of me. Forever and ever.

His muscles flexed with the long glide of his hips. Moving in and out, his pace picked up, and he threw his head back on a groan.

"Fuck, Everly, I need you to come with me, baby." He gripped my legs, bringing them up so they were bent at the knee, leaving me wide open to welcome in some unknown and raw place. He was hitting the heart of me, literally and figuratively. He found me and was making me feel everything.

I'd wanted to not feel anything when I'd come over tonight. This was going the opposite of that.

"Jackson." His name was a benediction falling from my tongue.

He growled, rough and jagged. What should have been sweet sent a flood of heat between my thighs as he entered me again. He groaned as he pulled out.

"Mine, so good, so fucking tight, perfect," became the soundtrack to the slow build of my orgasm, along with the pounding rhythm of his hips.

When I was stretched so thin, ready to break into a million pieces, I bit his shoulder so he would feel every ounce of pleasure I could give him.

Raking my nails down his back, I sunk them into the flexed muscles of his ass.

Shattering under his falling weight, I screamed his name and let go of everything but him, vaguely hearing his cry as he joined me.

We were one; we were us.

My breath shattered. He rolled over, and I splayed out onto his chest. His hands wrapped into my hair, holding me tight as our bodies calmed. Eventually, he pulled my lips to his, kissing me gently, looking at me like he couldn't believe his luck that I was here. We breathed into each other, sated.

"I think I'm doomed to love you even after I die," he whispered to me in the dark, the only time he ever seemed to give me his secrets.

"But maybe after death, it won't hurt so much to do it," I responded.

And we stayed like that, neither one of us moving, until morning.

14

"I'm the birthday bitch," Lane screeched loudly as she held up the bottle of champagne she'd been nursing exclusively for the last hour and danced on top of the tabletop of the club we'd come to in the city. Since I refused to attend any more school functions, because they were all starting to become dangerous to my health...and possibly my life, we'd skipped celebrating her birthday at the frats and had come to a club that one of her friends had connections with.

Hence the table service in a booth right near the dance floor.

I'd never seen Lane relax like this, and it made me a bit jealous of my best friend. What would It be like to feel that carefree for once? I tried to remember if I'd ever felt like that in my life. Maybe before my dad had killed himself, before my parents had started fighting over money.

But certainly not since then.

Besides Lane's good mood, the night was also looking up because there were no guys in our little group. I hadn't talked to Jackson since leaving his house two days earlier, although he'd tried to call and text me. Everything had been blissfully Caiden free, and I'd told Landry that I needed some time.

Maybe that was what I needed, some completely man-free time. I'd done it for the two years prior to coming to Rutherford Academy, and I'd never had to worry about being pushed down stairs, grabbed in a haunted house, or trapped in a shower with a snake.

Except as soon as the thought of taking a break from Jackson permanently popped in my head, I knew I couldn't do it. The other night had been special... More than special, it had been life-changing. Who knew all it took to stoke the obsession in my blood for Jackson was for him to throw in a little bit of the "L" word while looking deeply in my eyes?

Ugh. I was hopeless.

"Stop thinking about Jackson Parker," Lane screamed in my face drunkenly. "We need to dance."

Lane grinded in my lap, giving me my own personal lap dance, and I giggled while blushing like crazy.

"*No*," Lane suddenly groaned, and I groaned right along with her when I saw what she was looking at. A bunch of the hockey team had just walked through the doors of the club, led by Landry of course.

I had a hard time believing that his presence here was random.

I took a moment to observe him before he saw me. One of the hostesses was bringing them to a table near ours, and it was only a moment until he saw me.

Landry looked good tonight. He was wearing a forest green button up shirt and dark blue jeans. The green of his shirt made his hair and eyes pop, even in the dim lighting of the club. His hair was perfectly styled, and he was garnering stares as he walked with the team.

He'd taken the news that I wanted to cool off better than I'd expected, but I wasn't holding out that we could ever be "just friends" again. I watched as girls began to flock to the team as soon as they were seated, but Landry didn't do anything to encourage any of them. And the girls hovering around were gorgeous.

I pulled my eyes off Landry and snorted when I saw that Lane had found a brown-haired hottie and dragged him to our table, making him do shots that I'm sure she'd also made him pay for.

Black caught my gaze.

I frowned as a familiar looking head disappeared into the crowd beyond where I'd been watching Lane.

A head that looked like it belonged to Caiden.

I stood up, trying to look through the crowd and see if it was him, or if I was just imagining things. My heart threatened to fly away in my chest.

Of course, standing up put me in the direct sight of the hockey team's table...and Landry.

"Everly," called Landry, and I winced, before schooling my face and turning towards him with what I hoped looked like a pleased smile.

"Landry!" I exclaimed, trying to sound surprised. "What are you guys doing here? Don't you usually party at your frat?"

Landry had the decency to blush in embarrassment. "Krystal kind of told one of my teammates that you guys would be here, and I kind of convinced the team to come here tonight...hoping that you would talk to me."

My heart softened at his admission. Honesty was prized in my life, and Landry was always full of it.

"I'm glad you're here," I told him, surprised that I actually meant it.

He opened his mouth to say something, and then a pair of arms was hugging both of our arms like an octopus. Lane's head peeked in between us.

"Landry! Are you here for my birthday?" she called loudly, and Landry shot me an amused look. Lane drunk was kind of awesome.

"Happy birthday, Laney."

Her face brightened. "You have to take shots with me for my birthday. Everly babe, you're behind."

I groaned but sat back down at the table, with Landry's hand burning hot on my lower back as he sat down too.

"Oh, I forgot to tell you. You have to pay for them," Lane sang with a snort before curling up with laughter. Landry and I laughed right along with her.

Landry signaled the eager waitress, who did her best to flirt with him while he ordered some lemon drop shots.

They were delivered to the table quickly, and I winced as I shot one down and then another.

The last one tipped me over the edge. I was officially drunk, I decided, as the room seemed to glimmer in front of me. I grabbed a glass of water and gulped it down, calling it quits for a while until I got my feet back under me.

"Have I told you how much I love you and how pretty you are?" Lane asked drunkenly, stroking my face messily.

I was only faintly aware of Landry's arm now stroking the skin peeking out from under my black fringed halter top. "She is really pretty, isn't she, Laney girl," Landry agreed as his fingers dipped under the bottom of my tank.

More shots arrived at the table. "From those guys over there," the waitress said, pointing to Landry's team.

"I can't do anymore," I groaned.

"One more. One more. One more," Lane chanted.

"One more," I agreed as I chugged another glass of water for good measure before taking the shot.

"Did this come right from the bar?" I asked the waitress suddenly, a weird itch sliding up my spine.

"Brought them here myself," she said before hustling away.

Landry handed me one of the shots. "To Lane," he announced.

"To Lane!" our group shouted as we threw back the shots.

LANE WAS DANCING a hairsbreadth away from me, a blond hottie from the hockey team practically humping her from behind. Landry was behind me, his hands stroking across my stomach as he moved to the greatest song I'd ever heard. His arms had me caged against his body, and I wasn't complaining. Warmth spun across my skin as he pressed against me, two strong hands gliding over me.

I'd taken that last shot, and it must have done the trick, because I'd never felt better in my entire life. I was lost to the sensations, blissed out beyond measure. I felt Landry's hard length behind me, and nothing had ever felt so good. The room was spinning around me, a kaleidoscope of flashing lights that echoed the beat of the song.

My hands slid up his neck, into his gorgeous russet-colored hair. My whole body throbbed with need. The chemistry between Landry and I felt otherworldly, and I wanted him so fucking bad.

Landry trailed his lips along my jaw, and I moaned at the sensation. "Want to get out of here, sweetheart?"

"Mmmh," I moaned, my eyes half-lidded as I pushed to get closer to him.

I groaned when he stopped moving and began to walk me off the dance floor. I stumbled, almost falling, and he scooped me up in his arms and carried me the rest of the way.

"You feel so good," I whispered throatily as he dragged his lips along my skin while he began to walk us somewhere.

There was a gnawing pressure in the back of my mind, like I was supposed to be remembering something, but I just couldn't reach it.

Crisp air rushed across my face, and the cool air felt like heaven against my overheated body.

"Landry," I whispered, brushing my lips against his hand. He shivered beneath my touch. His skin was so soft. How did he get it so soft? I just wanted to rub myself against it, over and over again.

"You can rub yourself on me as much as you want, forever in fact, sweetheart," he growled.

I giggled. I must have said that out loud.

"Yes, you did," he said in an amused voice.

He shifted my weight, and I was faintly aware of his car door opening again. And then that gnawing sensation that I was forgetting something important hit me again.

I was laid down on something smooth and soft, and I rubbed against it, mumbling softly to myself about how tired I was.

"You're not going to sleep yet, Everly. I've got plans for you," said Landry as an engine rumbled to life around me.

"So tired," I responded, stroking the seat idly beneath my fingertips, trying to trace how I got here. I hadn't been that drunk, right? I'd had one, three, five shots?

The whole night was blurring together so much, but this cushion was so soft.

Just like Landry's skin as he massaged down my back, grabbing my ass and making me moan and grind into the cushion.

My body was on fire. I was on fire. I needed water.

"I need water."

"Soon, sweetheart." Landry's voice drifted to me.

The lull of the engine began to soothe me to sleep, until Landry slapped my ass, making me yelp in surprise.

"Stay awake, sweetheart."

Sweetheart. I hated when he called me that. Someone else called me something better. What was that again?

Little angel.

That's right.

Jackson. I wished Jackson was here.

Landry's hands felt so good though.

I heard a low growl, and then the vehicle we were in came to a sudden stop.

I didn't have a seatbelt on, and I flew forward off the front bench of the passenger seat, my body hitting the dash hard.

"Owww."

I was yanked back on to the seat, and a knee pressed between my legs until I had no choice but to spread them. Landry was above me, a fierce look on his face.

"Stop saying his name," he spit at me.

"Whose name?" I asked, confused. Something warm and wet slid down the front of my face, dripping into my eye. I reached up and looked at my hand in confusion when it came back with red stuff all over it.

That was mean of Landry to put ketchup on my head.

He suddenly pressed a punishing kiss on my lips, and it

hurt. But my skin was on fire. Everything on my body needed to be touched, or soothed, or fucked.

I didn't even know what I wanted.

"I'm going to fuck him out of your head, so you'll never mention his name again," Landry snarled, still talking for some reason about some mysterious person.

I felt him fumbling with the top of my jeans, and then the button was popped open.

What was Landry doing? Did I want him to do it? Landry was so handsome.

"That's right sweetheart. I'm so handsome. And you're so fucking beautiful. And you're mine. You're going to be mine."

Sweetheart. There was that word again.

Jackson.

Landry pulled my pants down, and I tried to remember why this was a bad idea and how I got here, but nothing seemed clear. It was like my brain had been stuffed with cotton.

And I was tired, so fucking tired.

I moaned in distress as he began to pull on my thong and then softly stroked a part of me that no one had ever touched besides Jackson.

Jackson.

What was happening?

I began to struggle underneath Landry, trying to tell him that he needed to stop, that I didn't want this, even though my body was completely arguing otherwise. Because every stroke of his hand felt so fucking good.

But that sensation in my head, the one that told me that something was wrong...it just kept growing, and even though everything felt amazing, I knew it wasn't supposed to be Landry who was doing it.

"Please," I cried softly. It felt like I was wading through butter. Was my body actually struggling, or was I just imagining it?

"I'll make you feel so good," Landry promised, sounding out of breath.

I started to go numb, like I was drifting above my body and watching as it happened to me.

The door behind Landry was suddenly ripped open, and Landry was torn off my body. I laid there, unable to move, but I could hear the sounds of fists hitting flesh and harsh yells.

It seemed to last forever.

And then a concerned, familiar face appeared above me, and a tear trailed down my cheek because I couldn't move anymore, I couldn't even move my lips to speak.

"It's okay, LyLy. I'm here. I'll never let anything happen to you again."

He gently pulled my underwear and pants back up my legs, and then his arms wrapped around me and pulled me off the car bench, and I was hoisted into his arms.

I could hear his familiar heartbeat as I leaned into his chest, his scent washing over me and trying to stir a thousand memories.

His heartbeat sounded like heartbreak. But I couldn't even move my head to get away from it.

What was Caiden doing here?

I was gone into the numbness before I could process another thought.

15

I leaned over and threw up, faintly aware of soft hands holding my hair back and whispering sweet nothings as I wretched over and over again into what looked like a pink bin.

I peeked open my eyes, a difficult venture since my eyes felt like they had been glued together by concrete, and a spark of pain crashed into me. I let out a silent scream, or at least I think it was silent, since I didn't hear the sound of glass breaking around me from the shrill sound.

I tried to breathe through my nose as nausea continued to hit me hard.

What had happened to me?

The night's events filtered slowly through my brain. We were at a club for Lane's birthday. Lane was shit-faced. Landry had shown up. We had taken shots.

What had happened after that? I remembered chugging water at some point. Had I drunk so much that I blacked out? That wasn't really like me.

There were bits and pieces slowly appearing in my

memory. But it was like what I was seeing had happened to someone else.

And why did my skin feel like it was covered in a thousand ant bites it was so itchy?

I heard murmured voices, but I'd given up on trying to open my eyes because the concrete glue on them felt too heavy.

But then I heard Caiden's voice murmuring to someone else in the room, and wouldn't you know...my eyes ripped right through that concrete.

Caiden was standing at the foot of my unfamiliar bed, talking to a woman dressed in scrubs.

I was at the hospital. And Caiden was here.

I wanted to cry, run away, do something.

I needed Jackson.

Caiden must have seen my distress, because he turned his attention away from the nurse and held up his hands cajolingly like I was a wild animal about to attack.

My whole body was trembling, and I started looking around the room for my purse so I could call someone...anyone.

Jackson.

The nurse finally moved her eyes from devouring Caiden's face and came over to me.

"Hey, sweetheart, glad you've woken up. You gave us all a scare."

Sweetheart.

The word spiked a thousand memories that I would pay anything to not remember. I wanted to think that the flashes I was seeing weren't real, but he'd touched me. I could feel his touch. And I didn't know why I'd acted like that. How had I drunk so much?

I began to weep, gut wrenching sobs, like I hadn't done since...well, since Caiden actually.

Was something wrong with me that I just didn't see things coming? Never in a million years would I have thought that Landry would do that. Never in a million years had I thought that Caiden would do that.

It was official, there was something terribly wrong with me.

But it still didn't explain how everything had happened tonight.

I didn't remember drinking so much.

"You were drugged," Caiden said quietly to me. He'd been watching me silently. I'd felt his hot gaze on me, and it made me want to tear off my skin.

"Drugged?" I repeated numbly, the words failing to register properly in my brain.

The nurse patted my hand. "A mixture of molly, Rohypnol, and ketamine. You're lucky to be alive, sweetie. Any stronger doses, and you would have been dead. It was the perfect combination."

I stared at the nurse in disgust. She sounded almost...impressed.

I started to cry again, because man, did it fucking suck that I didn't have a mom who I could call to help me right now.

I looked at Caiden through my tears. He looked devastated, like he could feel what I was feeling.

"Did Landry... How did you...?" I didn't know what questions to ask first. Everything was a tangled, jumbled mess, and I just wondered when I was going to catch a break, because honestly, it didn't feel like I could handle this.

He rubbed his forehead, like he always did when he was stressed, and I leaned towards the familiarity. "I was there with some guys from the team. It took me a little bit to connect the dots, but I saw him slip your waitress some money when he went to the bathroom just a few feet away from our table. I thought he was just tipping her or hell, paying her for sex later or something. But then when the tray of shots came to your table, he picked up a shot and kind of turned away from the group for a second, looking down at it. It was the one he gave you."

He took a deep breath, and I could almost hear the shame and regret in that breath. I braced myself for what he was going to say next.

"But again, I'm an idiot and I was a little bit drunk, so I didn't connect anything. Until you started acting so weird on the dance floor. I'd never seen you so..."

"So sexual?" I asked, my face flushing. Because I could remember now how good Landry's skin had felt against mine, how much I'd wanted him. How much that hadn't made sense.

"Yeah, that," he responded, shifting uncomfortably as his gaze flickered away from me briefly in embarrassment before returning. "When he walked you off the dance floor and then picked you up to take you out of the club, I finally came to my senses and knew something was wrong. I drove after you guys and reached you right before he was about to..."

"About to rape me," I finished for him in a whisper.

I felt...so dirty.

"I need to shower. And maybe call...Lane." I wanted to call Jackson, but I didn't feel like I could say that in front of Caiden. "Have you seen my phone?"

"I think you might have left it at the club because I haven't seen it. I didn't know who to call or have any numbers of my own to call."

"They're probably all freaking out."

"Jackson," Caiden commented, watching me intensely in that way that he always did since he'd come back.

"Lane," I corrected, although Jackson was probably freaking out as well. Maybe. We still had yet to have a conversation that didn't involve our bodies taking over.

But I couldn't ignore that the only person I wanted with me right now was him.

"I texted Jackson since that's one number I did have, but I haven't heard from him. For all I know, he blocked my number after everything though."

I didn't know what to say to that. Tearing them apart was something I'd actively tried to avoid from the beginning, but I couldn't deny that it felt good for the truth to be out there. I didn't know what I would have done if Jackson had found out the truth...and done nothing. It felt right for someone to fight for me for once, like I was a person who deserved to be fought for.

"How do you feel right now?" Caiden asked, approaching the chair next to me slowly, even though I could tell by how close it was to the bed that he'd already been sitting in it at some point.

"Terrible," I croaked. "And I just can't believe that Landry... I knew something was off with how I was acting, but it was like I was watching someone else, like I was existing outside my body." I started to cry again, my shoulders trembling. He reached a tentative hand out and took my hand in his, squeezing mine gently. Some of my tears fell on his skin, and his hand jumped like they'd burned him.

"Sorry," I mumbled.

"I'd forgotten how sweet your tears were," he whispered under his breath, almost like the comment hadn't been meant for me. And it shouldn't have been meant for me.

It was fucking creepy.

"You certainly saw enough of my tears over the years." I let go of his hand like it was poison and folded my arms, trying to hug myself and give myself the comfort that I needed right now, since there was no one else to give it to me.

Just like always.

"Is there something wrong with me? Am I just doomed for bad shit to happen to me over and over again?" I looked at Caiden, still watching me, like he could provide answers for the bad luck that seemed to follow me everywhere.

Caiden was mercifully silent.

I'd always wanted to believe that we were in charge of our own fate. My father had chosen to steal from all the people that had trusted him. He'd chosen to kill himself. My mother had chosen to be a selfish harpy, holding on to her past riches above all else.

But now I wasn't so sure about that.

I hadn't chosen to love Jackson and Caiden. My brain hadn't been an active participant in the journey. It was like there had been an invisible string connecting me to them all the time, leaving me with no choice. And then when my soul had changed the story, deciding that Jackson was the only one who could complete it...well, I hadn't had a choice in that either.

I wasn't so sure that I had a choice in my life anymore. And I was beginning to think that I'd done something wrong in a past life, because fate had been a total bitch to me lately.

The memory of Landry stroking my most intimate parts had me wanting to throw up again. I felt ruined.

"You're not ruined, LyLy. Nothing could diminish your

perfection," Caiden said firmly, and I realized I'd spoken the words out loud.

"Where's Landry now?" I asked, my gaze jumping to the door like I expected him to appear there at any minute.

"Hopefully hiding in a dark cave somewhere, because if I ever see him again, he'll regret the day he was born. I was so worried about getting you to the hospital that he didn't get what he deserved." He looked at me apologetically, like he'd done something wrong by choosing to save my life over seeking retribution.

I studied him, my gaze drifting over his features that I thought I might know better than I knew my own. The Caiden sitting here...he reminded me of the old him. The one I'd loved with all my soul...like a brother.

I wanted to fall into old habits, wrap myself around him and ask him to make everything all right. And for a second, I allowed myself to think about what would happen if I gave into the temptation. If I allowed myself to feel the warmth of his hug, to bask in his laughter, to look at him like he was the sun.

"Thank you for saving me," I told him, trying to hold onto that feeling that I knew so well, just for a minute longer. And I was grateful. If Landry had gone one step further, it might have been the end of me, the straw that broke my proverbial back. Who would have thought that Caiden would be the one to do that for me?

And so when he put his arm around me, I didn't lean away, even though my head was begging me to get out of the bed and run away as fast as I could. I allowed my heart to have a second to savor the feeling of someone whose embrace was almost as familiar as my own.

But then I pulled away and I saw the hunger in his eyes, and I was reminded once again how important it was for me to stay away, to keep up the walls that I'd spent the last two years building.

Because I'd once been the girl who'd believed in him, and there wasn't a day that went by that I didn't curse myself for being so blind with my trust.

A knock sounded on the door, and I cringed, because Jackson was standing at the door, a fierce and distrustful look on his face as he looked at his brother, who was still leaning towards me with a hand on my shoulder.

"Jackson," I sighed, his name like a prayer from my lips.

And then I burst into a fresh wave of tears. Jackson rushed over to me and pulled me into his embrace, and I buried my head in that spot between Jackson's neck and shoulder that I loved so much.

He let me cry for a long minute, softly stroking my hair like I was something fragile and breakable. I finally pulled away and realized that I was sitting in between Caiden and Jackson, something that hadn't happened for a really long time.

Another sob tore out of my mouth because I realized that it had once been my favorite place, and now I wanted to be out of the situation as fast as possible.

"So you guys are together?" Caiden asked at the same time that Jackson asked, "What did you do, fucker?"

"Let me remind you that I was the one who texted you," Caiden snarled, his upper lip curling with hate.

"He saved me," I said softly before things could escalate any more. "Landry..." The words got stuck in my throat. I still hadn't been able to wrap my mind around it. That Landry would do that, my mind just couldn't comprehend.

"The hockey player drugged her and then tried to rape her. I saw the end of it and drove after them. Luckily, he'd pulled onto a side road to make it happen and I was able to catch up to them."

"Landry?" Jackson snarled, his eyes widening.

And I realized that this was the kind of event that could set him into another episode.

I couldn't handle another episode right now. I couldn't take care of Jackson again right now, not when I needed someone to care for me.

Jackson must have seen the stricken, worried look on my face, and he took a few deep breaths, trying to calm himself down and stay with me.

"You can go now," Jackson said to Caiden in a much calmer voice, not bothering to look at him as he said it.

I could feel the fury rolling off Caiden in waves. And a little bit of guilt snuck in that he was being so casually dismissed when he'd just done this huge, life changing thing for me.

"Jackson, can you step outside for one moment?" I whispered, resigned to the fact that I was going to have to say thank you to Caiden at least one more time. I could examine closer what this meant a little later when I wasn't so emotionally…and physically shattered.

Jackson opened his mouth to argue.

"Please," I asked.

He shot Caiden a look of warning and stood up. "I'll be just outside," he threatened, before strolling out of the room. I could see his shadow coming in from the doorway, and it made me feel immeasurably safer.

When did that happen? I wondered. *When did Jackson begin to make me feel safe again?*

I turned my attention back to Caiden. His face was perfectly blank, and a wave of unease rolled across my skin at how easily Caiden was able to block his emotions. He was the master at it actually.

"I just wanted to thank you again. It means a lot," I told him. *More than I'm comfortable admitting.*

He stared at me inscrutably, and then his face broke and I was almost washed away with the depth of his emotions. Maybe it was better that he was able to hide what he was feeling so well, because I didn't think that I could handle seeing evidence of a love that had already destroyed me once before in my face constantly.

"I would do anything for you," he said softly...and there was so much affection in his voice that it was literally heartbreaking.

"I don't need you to do anything else. This was enough, Caiden." I didn't know whether I was reminding him that I'd forgiven him for that night two years ago, or if I was telling him that I didn't want to see him again. Both were equally likely with how I was feeling at the moment.

He nodded, like he'd understood whatever message I was trying to convey to him better than I'd understood it myself.

"I'll go ahead and get out of here. I desperately need some sleep," he said with a soft laugh, standing up and brushing his still too-long hair out of his eyes.

He gave me a sad smile and then walked towards the door. He stopped suddenly and turned around, a determined look on his face. "I don't want you to feel bad about what happened with Landry, Everly. Or think that you acted a certain way that made him do that to you."

I stared at him numbly. It was like he could read my mind.

"It's not anything you do, Everly. There's just something about you that drives a man to madness. Landry would have never had his fill of you…just like I haven't. You're irreplaceable. A man would have to die to ever escape your lure."

"I would turn it off if I knew how to," I told him desperately, needing him to know that I didn't mean to cause him this pain.

He gave me that same mournful, resigned smile once again. "I accepted my fate long ago, Everly."

And then he left the room.

I was staring blankly at the wall, shaking when Jackson rushed back into the room. "Are you okay? What did he say? Fuck, I shouldn't have left."

"I don't really know what he just said. I'm confused… about everything," I admitted, eagerly absorbing his beautiful face, even if it was marred by dark circles like he hadn't slept for days.

"Baby," he sighed, closing his eyes. "I think I've lived five lives since I got Caiden's text. Can you come back to my place when they release you this afternoon? I need you by me."

"They're releasing me this afternoon?" I said happily.

"Yeah, I just heard it from the nurse."

I rolled my eyes. "You know it's kind of amazing how easy it is as a Parker to get access to privileged medical information."

He smiled cockily, the sight making my soul sing.

The atmosphere changed, his eyes transitioning from ferocious to bewildered. "You're tearing me apart, baby," he mumbled.

Before I could reply, he leaned in so close our breath mixed. Closing his eyes, his lips found mine, slowly at first, a gentle exploration.

"I'm not broken," I murmured into him, and then my hands were in his hair. Pulling him from tentative to certain, he became insistent and pushed against me. Soft and firm all at once, he took his time to taste me in long licks, groaning as he did. My head didn't hurt so much as the empty ache between my thighs. This man, with his wicked tongue and beautiful mouth, one arm propped against the top of my bed so he could arch over me while freeing his other hand to skim the outside of my breast. A featherlight touch that I felt everywhere—a pang in my heart and a tempting pulse down my entire body.

Fuck. The hospital was not the place, nor was this the time to get distracted by the sexual attraction that apparently neither of us had the strength to ignore. Slowly we broke away, my fingers trailing down his jaw, which he clenched as they raked over his cheeks. Pressing his forehead against mine, I held him close while our breathing slowed.

The doctor arrived, and Jackson snapped up, moving to the corner of the small room.

"Ms. James, you got very lucky," he began disapprovingly. "I'm sure you've been warned not to take drinks from strangers, you could have died."

My cheeks flushed with shame, and I didn't bother to correct him with what had really happened. The truth was much more awful than that.

Jackson's fists were clenched and his jaw ticked, but he didn't say anything, controlling himself for once...something I was grateful for.

The doctor turned his attention to Jackson, taking a step back when he saw the ferocity written all over Jackson's face. "Watch for dizziness, blurred vision, a worsening headache, and vomiting. She'll be tired for the next few days as the drugs work their way out of her. I recommend waking her every few hours just to make sure she isn't having a latent reaction. If it seems like it's hard for her to wake up, call us immediately. If you want to go out and get your car up by the front, I'll send the nurse in with discharge instructions."

Jackson nodded, and the doctor left without a backward glance. The staff here really needed to work on their bedside manner.

Jackson grabbed my clothes and handed them to me. "Here, let me help you."

For some reason, the thought of him helping me get redressed out of my hospital gown had a flush spreading all over my chest. The guy had seen lots of my naked parts, but I felt somehow that it was more intimate for him to dress me than it had been for him to undress me.

"I'm not an invalid. I can dress myself. And I know what he said about you watching me, but I probably should get back to my room tonight. I'm sure Lane can come check on me once or twice." The words came out half-heartedly. It was like I was saying them just to see what his reaction would be.

Jackson studied me as if he was prepared to wrestle me down in order to win this battle.

"You know, we really need to break this habit of meeting up in hospital rooms," he suddenly said slyly, breaking the slow tension that had been building in the room.

"Shut up and get me out of here," I ordered.

He sidled up to me and grabbed my chin between his thumb and forefinger, tipping my head to find my eyes. The flare of his gaze was like a comet burning through a midnight sky. "You will be in my bed tonight, Everly. And there's going to be a time, not too long in the future, when my bed becomes your bed...permanently."

Holy... I nodded like he was a puppet master controlling my strings.

A laugh rumbled through his chest as he walked out of the room then with one last parting glance, leaving me with a stunned expression. I savored the rare sound of his laugh, a small smile on my face.

But as soon as he left the room, my smile dropped. Because that conversation with Caiden...it was churning in my gut. What Jackson was telling me was going to happen between us sounded a lot like forever, but Caiden's words had sounded a lot like forever earlier as well.

And Caiden's promises of forever had never meant good things for me.

16

My eye cracked open when a pounding from downstairs didn't stop.

"I know you're in there with her, Jackson Parker. You need to open this fucking door right fucking now," Lane called out from outside.

An unfamiliar voice yelled something from outside.

"Fuck you too, lady," Lane snarled at whichever of Jackson's neighbors were complaining at the way too early wake-up call.

Jackson groaned next to me. He'd woken me throughout the night with a soft caress to my cheek each time, unfortunately no sexy times happening in any of the wakeups. I would try something, and he would just smile and kiss my forehead.

Which was probably a good thing, judging by the fact that I could feel the pulse of a headache building again even now.

Jackson sat up next to me, the sheet sliding down his torso. His skin was burnished gold in the early morning light, and I had the insane urge to lick between his perfect abs.

"Good morning, little angel." His voice was sensual, warm, caramel smooth with a rough grate on the undertone from sleep.

If it was possible to melt, I did. My insides liquefied, and I leaned in towards him. It became infuriatingly easy to let the past disintegrate into nothing at the first pass of his mouth. A barely there brush, and then he tasted my top lip and then the bottom, teasing with his teeth. I groaned and closed my eyes, giving up the intimacy of watching for the relief of feeling. My hands roamed, steely biceps rippled under my touch, broad shoulders were just as rigid when he tightened his hold. His mouth was warm, tasting way too good, considering we'd just woken up, and destructive.

Long, provocative licks of his tongue rendered me speechless. Questions turned to need, and I dove into his hair to pull him even closer while I stroked back into his mouth. His growl rumbled between us.

I loved how his arms stroked along my skin. How did he do this? How could he make me so overwhelmed and desperate to attach myself to every part of him? I couldn't think; I could only feel. He was everywhere. His body and mouth commanded my response, and I responded by nibbling and sucking on his lips. We played until he broke away to nip my chin and neck.

"You're delicious." He pressed each word into my flushed skin.

"Quit fucking and open this motherfucking door," Lane yelled from downstairs, and I ripped away from him, feeling terrible for leaving her outside for so long.

Jackson's neighbors were probably going to start rioting.

I'd sent Lane a quick text on Jackson's phone the night

before, telling her that I was all right. I was sure she was in a panic from not having any more details.

"Your friend is annoying," Jackson commented as he dragged himself out of bed, flashing me a perfect view of his ass as he walked over to his dresser, completely nude.

I cursed the fact that I'd had Jackson Parker nude next to me and hadn't been able to take advantage of that. I really needed to stop having life-threatening events happen that led to his bedroom.

The joke sent a bucket of ice water crashing over me as Jackson pulled on a pair of pajama pants and left to go let Lane in.

Less than a minute later, the ball of energy that was Lane descended on me. She sobbed into my shoulder, squeezing me so hard, it was difficult to breathe.

"I'm going to kill him," she wailed, and I froze.

"You know?"

"Jackson told me."

"She let me get five words out before she was flying up here...into my bedroom," Jackson commented from the doorway, leveling Lane with an annoyed stare. "So I'm sure there are some blanks you can fill in...for both of us."

I shivered, dread licking up my spine at having to relive it. Lane finally let go of me and sat back, looking at me with raccoon eyes by her mascara smearing from her tears.

Haltingly, I told the story. Jackson had to leave the room halfway in, and I heard the crash of him hitting something against the wall. Lane scoffed at the noise and gestured for me to continue, her face becoming grimmer and grimmer as the story progressed.

"I'm going to kill him," Lane snarled when I'd finished. "I never liked that guy."

Now it was my turn to scoff. Lane had never outright said she didn't like Landry. Not that this was her fault at all.

Lane shivered and sniffled, rubbing her eyes again and smearing more mascara everywhere. "I'm never drinking again. I'm just going to attach myself to your side so you won't ever be alone."

"I'm never going anywhere but class, so that won't be a problem," I responded, although my heart lurched at the thought.

Before Caiden and Jackson had come into my life, I'd spent all my time in that big, decaying house with my mother. Except when I was in school, that house was all I'd known after my father had died. It seemed like a major step backward for me to once again be trapped in my room outside of class. And Melanie was almost as bad as my mother.

Lane's phone rang just then. Her face brightened as she picked it up. "I'll be right there to get it," she said before hanging up.

I looked at her expectantly. "The club found your phone. It had fallen under the table where we were sitting. I'll go get it."

"Thank you," I told her fervently. I hadn't even tried to explore yet what I was going to do to replace my phone if it wasn't found. I was the opposite of rolling in the dough at the moment.

Lane gave me a quick hug and jumped off the bed. "So... should I bring the phone back here?"

I opened my mouth and then closed it, not sure what the answer should be. I told myself a thousand times over that Jackson and I were done, and yet I always ended up here. I didn't think I could ever trust this new easiness between us, because it had happened after he read my journal and

Heartbreak Lover

found out the truth. If he hadn't found it, things would have continued on.

And even though the hate sex had been life-altering, the fact that Jackson's actions had reminded me every day that who I was wasn't enough for him was something I couldn't get over.

"I don't know," I finally said.

"She'll be here," came Jackson's voice. He stepped into the room, holding an icepack to his bloodied knuckles. Evidently, that noise earlier had been the sound of his fist hitting the wall.

"Excellent," Lane said excitedly, and I rolled my eyes.

Jackson and I locked gazes then, as Lane waved and hurried out of the room.

A million words were exchanged in that silence, and all of them were laced with *I love you...*

"Why don't you get cleaned up, and after Lane gets back with your phone, I want to take you somewhere."

"Where?" I asked suspiciously. He was looking at me like I was the sun, the moon, and everything in between.

He rolled his eyes. "Just shower," he ordered. "I have to go run a quick errand, but I'll be right back."

I resisted the urge to ask him where he was going like the needy girl I was unfortunately turning into. I watched as he went into his closet for a few seconds before coming back out in a tight-fitting black T-shirt and jeans that left little to the imagination.

I stuck out my tongue at him, even though what I wanted to do was lick him, and then walked stiffly to the bathroom. I was feeling a lot better, but man, if I needed one more reason to never do drugs, this was it. The after effects were killer.

I heard the garage open and close beneath the floor, and

I turned on the shower, hating myself because I already missed him.

Jackson

"Do you have him?" I asked Kyle, a starting linebacker on the team.

"Yeah we picked him up at his dorm room. We checked his phone, and the fucker had been trying to get in contact with Everly for hours."

"I'm on my way."

"Want us to start?"

"Nah, I need this to be very personal."

Kyle laughed darkly, knowing exactly what I meant, and we hung up.

Landry Evans was a dead man.

There was a football house a few blocks away from campus. Unlike the frat most of us were a part of, this was a house the alumni had bought the team, where the more clandestine shit went down. The hazing we didn't want to get reported, the assholes various members of the team needed to deal with...all the stuff the administration didn't need to know about.

I hadn't really had a need for the house until now.

But blood was about to be spilled. And I didn't want any additional eyes on what I was about to do.

I walked inside the ostentatious brick colonial that was the "football house." It was way too much for a bunch of college students, but nothing's too good for Rutherford Academy's football team. Our alumni had more money than Midas, and they were very generous with the team.

I've been grateful for the top-notch stadium, coaches, and training facilities since I'd been here. But today, I was very grateful for this house. Especially the basement portion of the house, which currently housed the cockroach that was Landry Evans.

The air got stale as I walked down the stairs into the basement. A few members of the team that I was close with stood watch, and they had Landry trussed up like a Thanksgiving turkey in a fold-up chair in the middle of the room.

It was a little bit too mafia looking for my tastes, but I guess whatever got the job done. As soon as I'd heard what Landry did to Everly, I'd arranged for him to get picked up. My body had been craving violence on Everly's behalf ever since my fight with Caiden. It was like my body idiotically thought that it could prove its worth to Everly by destroying as many of her enemies as possible.

Everly had goodbye in her eyes, and it was all I could do to hold on to her right now. But I would do whatever it took to stack the cards on my side.

Landry's eyes widened when he saw me, and then he schooled his features quickly.

"Why am I not surprised?" he spit out, brave for someone sitting tied up in a chair. But no one ever accused Landry of being smart.

Calculating maybe, the way he laid in wait for Everly to show some weakness, but not smart. He obviously let his dick do most of the thinking, since he'd had to pull off to the side of the road to try and force his way into Everly's pants instead of waiting to get somewhere private.

Hot rage curled in my stomach at the thought of what had happened.

I carefully tucked Caiden's part in the story away for a time when I could examine it more closely, along with the way he'd been looking at her when I'd walked into her hospital room. I didn't want to think about Caiden rescuing Everly right now. I couldn't handle it.

I circled Landry, just watching him. A small smirk lifted the corner of his mouth as he tipped the chair back on its back legs like he didn't have a care in the world.

I knew what would happen if Everly were to turn Landry in. It would be the same thing if some girl tried to turn me in, not that I would ever have to stoop to those levels to get laid. The police would slap the asshole on the wrist and then let him go with something that amounted to nothing. Or if they did pretend to take her story seriously, Landry's parents would drag her through the mud every day for the rest of her life. They'd call her a slut and slander her name until Everly wished she'd never said something to begin with. That was what happened for rich entitled guys like Landry. That was what happened for rich entitled guys like myself...and Caiden.

I saw Caiden sitting in that chair. Caiden had used his charm and resources to put the blame on Everly, so no one dared to suggest that maybe the poor girl from the bad family's injuries weren't all from that car wreck. Although thinking back now, that should have been obvious to any medical professional. But yet no one questioned Caiden because he was a Parker.

Not even me.

So that was why Landry was here. That was why I was here. Because while the legal system of this town might be wrapped around Landry Evan's proverbial dick—and that of every other guy just like him—I was not. Seeing him sit there with that smirk, knowing that he'd been trying to contact Everly even after what he did...hatred that I'd only ever felt before with Caiden simmered in the pit of my stomach, begging for release.

The possessive, obsessive love I had for Everly demanded nothing less.

"Man, I feel special. I've got the campus celebrity, Jackson Parker, here to see me," he said in a guttural drawl. "I bet you love this, don't you? I was so close to having your girl, and now she's going to run into your brother's arms."

A growl ripped from my throat. "Watch your fucking mouth. Don't mention her again."

Landry laughed, a manic look in his eye, and Kyle stepped forward. I held up a hand to stop him.

I stood over Landry. His chair lost its precarious perch, and the resounding thud of his skull as it hit the cement floor was music to my ears.

I wrenched my fist in his shirt, knocking his head against the floor another time so that his eyes looked slightly dazed and out of it. I then dragged the chair upright once again.

"Do you dream of how she tastes, how she smells? I have ten pairs of her used panties, and I've jacked off to them so much you can't even tell what color they are," he said with a dreamy look on his face, as if he were thinking about her perfect pussy right there.

There was little time between the movement of his mouth and my hand making contact with it. I hit him with so much force that blood painted the wall and floor behind him. All the anger living inside of me since I first heard what Caiden did was freed upon the bastard who tried to take what was only mine. A resounding roar escaped my throat when I connected again, this time splitting my already torn up knuckles on his cheek bone.

His scream was driven into a grunt as I lit into him again

and again. One side and then the other, until Kyle pulled me away, holding my upper arms back in a vice grip.

"You probably shouldn't kill him, Parker," Kyle drawled loud enough so that I could hear him above my jagged breath and Landry could start to fear what the end result of all of this was going to be.

Shrugging him off, I straightened my shirt, never taking my eyes off Landry. I'd made a mess of his face, a cracked lip and cheek, and I knew that the crazed smile on my face must've been a sight to behold. But I'd been carefully walking the line between normal and psychopath for years. It felt good to step over that line every once in a while.

"Is this all still a game to you? Are you still thinking about her underwear now, you sick fucker?" I dragged in a lungful of air, not expecting more than the moan he returned. "We're going to do this a bit longer. And then maybe I'll let you walk out the door. But so help me..." I lunged forward to grab him again and shook him so hard that his neck snapped backwards. "If you so much as think her name again, I will fucking end you."

Landry huffed out a breath, sputtering through his blood-tinged spit. "You don't deserve her..."

I smiled and crouched down in front of him. The hanging lamp swaying above my head painted the basement in a macabre light. I was sure Landry was shitting himself. "I don't care that I don't deserve her. She's mine. And this...this is me protecting what's mine. Now let's get started so I can get on with my life and get back *my girl*."

The look of hate and jealously he threw me let me know that he still hadn't gotten the message.

I laid a few more punches to his face for fun, and then I took a knife out of my pocket and held it right above his groin.

"What-what are you doing?" he stammered, a lisp to his words, thanks to the teeth that were missing.

"Giving you a reminder of what would be the first to go if you ever get close to Everly again." With those words, I sliced right above his dick, deep enough to scar, ensuring that he would be reminded of me and my warning for the rest of his life. I savored the screams filling the air.

I must have gone a bit too far, because he passed out from the pain, slumping over in his chair.

I straightened up and wiped my knife off on his pant leg. I glanced over at my teammates, and they looked a little bit scared of me.

Good. They'd make sure to stay away from Everly as well.

"You guys can get this cleaned up?" I asked, and all of them nodded quickly. "See you at weights tomorrow."

I left the room, and I was struck by just how gone I was.

There wasn't anything I wouldn't do for Everly James. My fate lay in her hands. I wanted to sink into her drowning softness and never recover. She was pure and good and everything I needed to be happy.

It was time to get back to Everly and put the next phase of my plan into action.

17

Everly

Lane had just dropped off my phone, and there were a million messages and voicemails waiting for me, which was rare because usually the only person to ever use my number was Lane...or my mother when she got particularly drunk and needed money from me. I'd spent the last hour trying to decide if I should go back to my dorm or not, but finally I'd given up and just decided to go through my phone.

I cringed when I saw that there were ten texts and five voicemails Landry had dared to leave me after what he did. I deleted them all without listening to them, knowing that I should probably keep them for evidence or something, but just wanting to remove everything about him from my life so I didn't have to think about it.

The next message I saw was from Caiden. I didn't know how he'd gotten my new number, but I'd never forget Caiden's number.

Want to get breakfast?

A sick feeling bubbled up inside of me. I didn't want to get breakfast with him, but did I owe him breakfast? Were we even now, or was I still in the red because of the two years of his life he'd lost because of me?

I replied before I could think any more on it.

Sorry. I already ate.

He replied back immediately.

Dinner then. I want to make sure you're okay.

He didn't include the question mark this time, and I knew he'd done that deliberately. The bastard was trying to leverage the fact that he'd saved my life to get back into it. In a way, I'd needed this kind of sign. He'd acted so like the old him that I'd needed a reminder that Caiden was capable of manipulation like none other.

Maybe the old Everly would have eagerly fallen into his offering, just grateful that Caiden Parker was paying attention to her.

But I wasn't that person anymore.

I would carry the regret of what had happened between Jackson, Caiden, and I for the rest of my life.

But it would be a cold day in hell before I let Caiden Parker back into my life.

My phone buzzed again.

Caiden: Pizza sound good?

Me: Sorry, I can't.

Caiden: Can't or won't?

I took a deep breath, trying to build up the courage to respond as I knew I needed to.

Just then I heard the garage open, and then a minute later, Jackson walked in, using his shirt to wipe down his body. Not quick or well enough to hide the fact that there was blood flecked all over his skin.

I knew immediately where Jackson had been. And I

knew that Landry Evans wasn't going to be anything but a bad memory from now on.

It was demented at how good it felt to know he'd sought the vengeance on Landry that I could never have gotten on my own. A warm feeling spread through my body, working its way through my veins and bloodstream until the feeling hit my heart, warping and shaping it until Jackson was all it could see.

I'm thankful for what you did, but I meant what I told you the other day. Let me go.

I fired off the text before I could change my mind and marveled at how light I felt having sent it. Three dots signaled that Caiden had read my text and was responding, and then they disappeared. The silence felt like bliss.

Jackson came to a screeching halt when he saw me sitting there, and I knew he must have thought I would still be upstairs...hell, or even gone when he'd walked in by the bashful, somewhat ashamed, look on his face as he watched my gaze dance all over his crimson streaked skin.

Something was wrong with me obviously, because I suddenly had an image of his blood-streaked body bending over mine, moving in and out of me with passionate thrusts until I was covered in Landry's blood as well.

I shook my head to clear it of my insane thoughts.

"Thank you," I whispered before he could say anything or try to apologize for what he'd done.

A fierce protective look crossed his face. "Always," he swore to me.

And for the first time in over two years, I believed a promise that came out of Jackson Parker's mouth.

"I just need a quick shower, and then we can go," he told me. His hands were clenching repeatedly like he wanted to tie me to a chair to make sure I didn't go anywhere.

But he didn't need to worry about me running...or walking as it were. I'd lost the desire to run, his blood-soaked skin a sacrifice that I didn't know I needed.

"I'll be here," I told him throatily, and a satisfied smirk curled on Jackson's lips. Of course, the asshole would see right through me right away.

He'd always seen me.

I sat there, mindlessly watching an episode of *Vampire Diaries*, when Jackson came down the stairs, looking sinfully delicious in fitted black jeans and white T-shirt that was stretched across his chest.

I stood up, fiddling with the edges of my shirt, because it seemed like we were about to go on a date, and in all my years with Jackson, we'd never been on a date.

Jackson prowled towards me until he was right in front of me, his eyes blazing with a smoldering need.

He walked me back until I was leaning against the wall. Jackson closed me in with his arms and then his mouth. For one second, I relaxed into relief at the stroke of his tongue, but then I ripped away, forcing my head to the side, panting. I was determined that we weren't going to get waylaid by sex today. At least not before the date even happened.

His rock-hard leg was pressed between my thighs, rubbing against me, and it felt so damn good. My body responded with a gluttonous flush that I felt from the top of my head down to the tips of my toes.

He sighed and leaned his forehead against mine. Beneath the cocky bravado, there was so much sadness in him. It was in me too, but I wondered for the first time if it had to be that way forever. If together, we might not be able to figure out a way through all the bullshit, that although not a happily ever after for most people, might be a happily ever after for us.

But that was just crazy talk. Right?

He leaned against me for a long moment more before he moved back and took my hand, dragging me towards the garage and then into his truck.

"So, are you going to tell me where you're taking me?" I asked as we set off down the road, my favorite James Arthur song playing softly in the background.

"You're still terrible at surprises," he remarked with an amused grin thrown my way.

I thought about it for a moment, and a big grin spread across my face. "Yeah, I guess I still am."

I laughed giddily at the thought that there was still something about me that was the same as the girl he once knew. Jackson did still know parts of me, even though he still had a long way to go to get the whole picture.

It was a relief quite frankly.

I managed to keep my impatience to a minimum, and when he turned out of town and set off down a literal red, dirt road that led into the woods, I bit my tongue and didn't ask him if he was taking me out in the middle of nowhere to kill me.

Because we were past that point, right?

The woods blocked out almost all traces of sunlight as the trees stretched over the road. Jackson drove a little farther down and then pulled off to the side of the road.

"You okay with walking a little bit?"

"Yeah," I responded, definitely intrigued by now.

Jackson grabbed a picnic basket from behind his seat that I hadn't seen him place there, and then he grabbed my hand, as was apparently his way now, and he started to lead me into the woods.

We walked through the forest, Jackson holding on tightly to me for around a mile. I was just about to tell him that my leg couldn't take it anymore when the tree line suddenly broke, and I stepped into a scene that I couldn't have imagined, even on my best day.

It was a field of wildflowers that stretched on for at least half a mile. Flowers of all colors, shapes, and sizes covered every square inch of the ground. Explosions of riotous color and sweet smells overwhelmed my senses, until it was all I could think or feel.

It was the most beautiful thing I'd ever seen.

But then Jackson turned to look at my reaction, and I saw him standing there, a golden god with the sunlight dancing across his features...and I had to amend that thought.

This field was the second most beautiful thing I'd ever seen.

Jackson Parker, stepping into the light from the darkness definitely took the top spot.

"What do you think?" he asked almost shyly.

"If I'd known a place like this existed, I would have done everything I could to spend as much time as possible here," I admitted. "It's beyond words."

A boyish grin lit up Jackson's face, and he closed his eyes and turned it up to the sun. It was like the field of flowers had stripped away all the shadows he usually carried, and before me was standing a Jackson who'd been freed.

What I would give to see him like this always.

After a long moment, where I just watched as the wind brushed across his golden hair and the light caressed his face, Jackson opened his eyes, smiling wider when he saw that I was watching him.

"Come on," he told me, taking my hand again and leading me right into the center of the field.

Opening up the picnic basket, he pulled out a blue

checkered blanket and spread it carefully on the ground. I watched in amazement as he pulled out at least ten plastic dishes and then a bottle of wine and two plastic wine glasses.

"I thought about trying to make us dinner, but then I thought we might want to enjoy our meal, so I ordered from Caputo's."

I laughed and settled myself down on the blanket, ignoring the way my leg groaned in protest.

Jackson had ordered my favorite chicken salad dish with pecans and red grapes, croissants, a vegetable plate, a Caesar salad, and their specialty white chocolate cranberry cookies for dessert. It was enough food for five people, and I couldn't wait to dig in.

Jackson poured us both wine, and then we ate quietly, admiring our surroundings and listening to the birds chirp around us.

It was like I'd stepped into a Disney movie. I'd never seen something so perfect, and I never wanted to leave.

"How did you find this place?" I finally asked when I'd finished stuffing myself with the delicious food.

"I needed to get away one day, so I decided to go for a drive. And I swear, it was like magic, because I was just driving along, and I got the urge to stop at the side of the road and go for a walk. I felt like an idiot walking through the woods without a trail or a plan, and then I stepped through the trees and I knew I was meant to find this place. Every time things just become too much, I come out here. No matter the season, there's always some kind of flower blooming here. It's my favorite place in the world."

"Mine too," I whispered, entranced with his story.

"Can I tell you something, and you not run away?" he

asked intently, staring at me as if my answer held the key to his entire world.

I hesitated before answering, because I felt like a flight risk in many ways when it came to him and I was afraid of the truths that could potentially come out of his mouth.

I took a look around though, and decided to pretend that nothing bad could happen in a place as lovely as this.

He scooted closer to me, getting up on his knees and settling in right in front of me so that our faces were only a few inches apart.

"I'm going to marry you here one day. I stepped into this field that first time, and that was all I could think. I saw you in a long white dress, your champagne curls streaming behind you as you ran to me. And even though I thought I hated you, didn't even know when or if I'd see you again, I knew after seeing this place that was our only fate. You. Me. And a field of wildflowers where I promise to love you until the end of time."

A tear slipped out of my eye and trailed down my face, and Jackson tracked its course until it dripped off my chin.

I could see that day. It made sense that I'd be running towards him, because all my life, I'd always been running towards him—wanting him, loving him, needing him.

So why when he was telling me that his dream was the same as mine, did it feel a little like heartbreak instead of redemption?

"Did I scare you away?" he asked as he gently touched the wetness on my cheek.

"I'm just wondering why you're saying the words that I've dreamed about probably since I met you, and yet I'm crying," I admitted.

"This place was a sort of new beginning for me. I'd been close to spiraling permanently before I found it." He took my hand in his and looked into my eyes earnestly. "I was hoping that this place could be a sort of new beginning for us. A starting point for a future together."

His words were beautiful, what any girl would want to hear. But I couldn't forget, wouldn't forget, that all of this was happening *after* he'd found out the truth. What if all we were meant to be was a sad, beautiful, tragic love story that would serve as a cautionary tale for our grandchildren one day, of what could happen if love burned too bright?

There was also the fact that in a way, we were strangers. The last few years had changed me so much, and it was obvious he had changed too. But while I was by myself, trying to piece myself back together, Jackson had been welcomed with open arms into Rutherford, treated as a football god. He couldn't relate to my journey, not in a million years.

"I'm struggling with the fact that all of this is coming *after* you found out the truth," I admitted quietly, my gaze drifting to some cherry-colored petals that were dancing in the wind. "You left me all alone, abandoned me after the single most traumatic event of my life." My breath hitched. "You should have believed me. I'd just shared this huge part of me with you. And even after that...you didn't believe me." I finally dragged my eyes back to his mournful gaze, tears heavy in my voice as I finished. "I'm afraid that if I take this step, all that's waiting for me is regret. I'm afraid that I'm in love with the ghost of you instead of who you are now. And I'm afraid that once you get to know who I am, who I am really and not who you've built up in your head, that you'll be immeasurably disappointed."

My confessions were heavy on my tongue, the dark secrets I'd never let see the daylight. For all those years, I'd done my best to give Jackson and Caiden only the highlights. I hid from them the darker parts of my soul, afraid that if I gave them something too honest, they'd run from me when they realized who I really was. Time hadn't changed who I was at my core, a girl who'd been abandoned by every significant figure in her life. I was damaged, a mirror that had been broken into a million pieces. And no matter how much love Jackson tried to give me, there would always be cracks under my skin that could never be fixed.

"I picked you before I knew the truth," Jackson replied, and my eyes widened in disbelief.

"Don't lie to me, Jackson. Not now, not after everything."

"I'm not lying. I'd decided when you left me in the library that I would do anything to get you back. Even when I found out that Caiden had woken up, I still had decided to pick you, no matter the consequences. I would burn the whole world for you, pick you first every time. You just have to give me the chance to do it."

I opened my mouth to object, and he laid a finger on my lips before hurrying on.

"If you give me one last chance, I swear on my life I won't let you down again. I know what I did is unforgivable, but, Everly, my heart is yours. You are what I hold onto. My first thought in the morning, my last thought when I close my eyes to sleep. I've dreamed about you every night since the last time I saw you in that hospital room. No matter how much time passed, I couldn't erase you. I feel like I've been carrying an open wound in my chest where I tried to remove you, but it never worked. You can't erase someone that's a part of your soul, Everly. Believe me, I've tried. You're meant for me. I'll protect you, I'll help you, I'll care for you, because you're meant for me. No matter what you say, no matter what you've heard. This is meant to be, and I'm not stopping until you give us a chance."

He leaned forward and pressed the softest, most perfect kiss on my lips. No one would ever think that the heartbreak prince could ever give someone that kind of kiss.

But that was because the heartbreak prince had never tried to give someone his heart.

That kiss, that perfect kiss...it did what his words couldn't.

My broken heart, the one that I thought could never be fixed?

It started to beat again.

And it beat just for him.

He saw it in my eyes, and a silence followed, the kind of silence that only two people who really understand each other can have. We went back and forth, watching each other and watching the flowers change color under the light of the shifting sun.

The silence stretched between us was broken when Jackson laid me down among the wildflowers. He took a deep breath, like he was breathing in bravery.

"Everly, I love you," he whispered.

And I believed him.

Tears pooled in my eyes, and I bit my bottom lip, trying to hold back the bigger tears that I wanted to cry. He cradled my face, tipping my head back and brushing a kiss over my forehead and cheeks, my nose and chin. He hovered over my mouth and took a deep breath and then another. Without any protest from me, he slid off my red tank top and jeans. His touch was tender as he caressed my body with the tips of his fingers and his eyes. He stripped me bare emotionally and literally, until I lay there naked beneath him, the act of removing my clothes one piece at a time somehow more intimate than all the times before.

My stomach did a somersault, and then suddenly, I was

pressing my face into his chest as I cried, really cried, like I hadn't before.

At once, my hands that were limp on the ground raged against him, fisting in his shirt and wailing against the hard muscle beneath, all the while he whispered in my ear, "I'm sorry, I'm so sorry, baby. I love you. I love you. I love you, Everly."

In time, the well finally ran dry and we just stayed pressed together, my sniffles the only thing interrupting the serenity between us. With fingers in my hair, he pulled until my head was tipped back and I was forced into eye contact. "I love you. I should have told you every day."

A look of vulnerability appeared on his face just then. "Do you love me?" He laughed bitterly. "I guess all of this means nothing if you don't."

"The fact that I love you might be the only thing I've ever really believed in in my entire life," I told him shyly.

"Say the words, little angel," he ordered, hope blossoming across his face.

"I love you," I told him with a quiet giggle.

"Again."

"I love you. I love you. I love you. I love you."

He kissed me, breathless, and when my lips were free, I added, "Always."

"Mine," he said as the perfect pitch of his hips against mine started to send every nerve into a tingling sense of awareness. "No more running. For either of us."

"No more running," I agreed.

Careful and sure, his next kiss was at first a gentle caress. He savored me, slow and sinful. A tilt of his head, a brush of his mouth, a tug from his teeth, the slightest hint of his tongue, and repeat until I was breathless. This was the kind of kiss that could last for days, and just when I settled in, he became reckless. From careful to careless, he licked into my mouth. Asserting his power, his fingers tugged at my hair and dove in. I moaned when his teeth pierced my bottom lip. The color of my voice painted the sky, matching the vibrant colors of the flowers around us, giving life to the still air.

One of my hands landed in his hair, and I pulled myself up and into him. The other gripped the front of his shirt. Twisting a handful of the cotton in my fist, I held nothing back, molding my body into his. I circled my hips, until his groan mirrored my own. He hurriedly stripped off his shirt, giving me a sexy-ass smirk as he did so.

Bare chest heaving, he kneeled above me, drinking me in with those insatiable, blue eyes that matched the sky above his head.

He didn't speak; he didn't have to. I could see everything written in the tight clench of his jaw, the tension easing as his gaze lingered over my body. He wanted me, but it was more than that. More than need, more than lust. The shadow covering his face was not enough to hide his love.

An unexpected moan escaped my parted lips, and my body was on fire just from his gaze. He smiled a feral smirk that grew as he crawled over me until we were nose to nose. I licked my lips and accepted his mouth when he crushed his against mine. I'd hungered for him constantly since that day I'd seen him in the Rutherford hallway, and it ate away at me whenever we were apart. I was desperate for his touch like never before. I felt his answering moan in the pulse between my thighs. It wasn't enough; it was never enough.

Not with Jackson.

Snaking my hand between us, I fumbled with the zipper of his jeans and settled for palming his erection through his pants. His mouth became more urgent, as did his tongue and hands. But he broke away, pushing up to his knees and pressing mine apart with the spread of his. The harsh sound of our labored breathing fell around us like the tails of a fireworks display—explosive and ready to start a fire.

Trying to take back a little control, my fingers glided over his length, and I squeezed at the base. Jackson was hot as hell, and all mine. My own personal golden god.

A lock of hair had fallen on his forehead, no doubt released from its perfection by my grip. I wanted him everywhere. I want to become overwhelmed by Jackson Parker, my mouth filled with the taste of him on my tongue, blinded by his beauty and held captive by his touch. "Please…"

"Please what?"

"Touch me."

Tipping his head back, he looked up at the fathomless blue sky while exhaling a deep breath. Sliding his knees further apart, he took mine with them, leaving me open and vulnerable. Being open with Jackson like this was like freedom. I didn't have to think or second guess what this was anymore. I just had to feel and take in each sensation and revel in the pleasure that followed. I wasn't embarrassed or self-conscious. I got to want, to need, to demand.

"Now," I ordered.

Gripping him harder grabbed his interest, and then he was on me, biting and kissing into my neck until I could barely remember my name. His teeth clamped onto my nipple. I bowed from the ground with the unexpected voracity with which he fed on me. His mouth had a direct line to the apex of my thighs, and he sucked until the ache between my legs was deep and pulsing, and then he flicked me with the tip of his tongue. I gasped as his teeth sunk in.

Covering me with his branding bites, he left what I was sure was a long path of impressions, first on one breast and then the other. But he wasn't done. Starting again, he sucked and lapped at my chest until my nipples were screaming, or maybe I was, from sensitivity.

More, I need more, and I needed him to touch me everywhere, but he followed his design, matching them and deepening the marks that would surely last a lifetime...if I was lucky.

It wasn't just my groin that pulsed in a torturous ache, but my skin. My breasts were hot and heavy under his attention, yet the heat had traveled along every nerve, and they were begging for the wet glide of his tongue and piercing imprint of his teeth. I'd never loved and hated the cool air of the breeze blowing across us so much in my life. It was an aching blow. I longed for it, wanted to feel the echoes of the rush and the sting as it skimmed over my newly formed imprints that drove both pleasure and pain. They bound me, as surely as I was bound to him.

Whimpers fell from my lips, one after the other, mixing with Jackson's hungry groan as he licked his way to my navel. He was greedy and impatient as he moved down my body, until he got on his knees and spread my thighs open wide.

Holding me down with a hand on each one, he stared at me through his lashes. "I'm obsessed with your taste, your cries, everything about you."

A scream burst out of me when he dipped down. That tongue. I loved his fucking tongue.

He flicked my clitoris, and we both moaned. His teeth and lips, and...and... Holy shit... His mouth hollowed out when he took me in without mercy.

"Yes," I gasped. I gripped his hair, holding him in place as an orgasm took over, and I lost a little bit of my sanity in the white-hot bliss that surrounded me.

Just when I thought he'd let up, when his tongue replaced his teeth and the long slide of it eased against the peak of my high, he started again. Ravenous and demanding, that beautiful mouth was still hungry against me. Involuntary jerks took hold of my muscles as I spasmed beneath him. His hand snaked out and grabbed my breast, pinching it so the ache wasn't only centered under his lapping tongue, but all around the depraved branding he gave me moments ago.

"Again," he mumbled into me, his eyes sharp as they pinned me down.

"No," I cried and wrenched away, but he followed without missing a beat and a pinch of his teeth. "Oh...Jackson."

"Yes," he growled, forcing his demand into my flesh as he worked me over. I was lost in the graze of his mouth, and this time when he took me in, his fingers, first one and then another, sunk inside, finding the spot, the amazing I'm-never-going-to-recover-from-this spot, he rubbed in and out, over and over.

"Stop, please," I begged as my knees drew up and locked around his head. But he didn't let go. He just kept licking and sucking and...I let go.

I gave in to the pleasure at his insistence and welcomed the numbing paralysis that seized and drew me from the ground and into the arch of a dancer, graceful and poetic. My arms followed the pose, lifting above my head in the rigid form needed to hold the frame as I spiraled out of control.

My breathing was suspended, as was the scream immortalized with my statue-like position. Oh, so amazing. As I came down, he pulled me up and onto his waiting lap. Without thought, I straddled his knees, and just when my fingers found their place in his hair and my arms wrapped around his head, he glided inside of me.

The stretching fullness, the pulsing depth, the mind-altering moment when we were one stopped time, and he gave me that minute to just feel him.

"Little angel, you feel so good."

I was complete and wanted for nothing.

Then it changed. My body took charge and demanded movement.

"Hold on, baby. I'm going to give you everything."

He gripped my hips, lifting only to buck up as I sunk down in a slick, frantic stroke. Again, up and down. I whimpered as his mouth found mine, dipping in long, licking strokes, until we were both gulping for breath.

"Yes," he whispered into my skin, "tell me what you want."

"I want this forever," I gasped and let my head fall back. Hands resting on his shoulders, I found the arch, the pose that stretched me thin and pulled out every ounce of pleasure my body could reap from his. Jackson's growl spiked my lust.

I became wild, finding the feral side he brought to the surface not too long ago. Our bodies came together in violent slides of wet and heat and hunger. Leveling my eyes to his, I sunk my nails into his back and said, "I want you to come."

"Fuck," he choked out as I pushed him down, and we rolled so he was on top. His teeth found their place on my neck as he sunk in, a long, hard glide.

Oh, shit.

He'd driven me into a frenzy. I couldn't get enough. Please. This wasn't supposed to happen again. It couldn't be this intense, but it was, and oh...Jackson.

"Make me come with you," he groaned and lifted up on his hands above me, working his hips faster, pushing deeper as my legs rounded his ass. Sweat beaded on his brow and along the strong line of muscles that bunched and pulled with exertion throughout his entire body. I was coiled like a spring, and any minute, with the next thrust, oh...yes. I jerked beneath him and then around him as pleasure ripped through me.

"Fuck, oh fuck, baby, I can feel you." He threw his head back and lost himself, taking over my wildness and bucking into me as everything else disappeared. I welcomed him in my arms when he fell into his own heaven.

"I love you," I whispered and kissed into his shoulder. "I love you so much."

Tears clouded my vision, derived from the beauty before me, and the experience we'd just shared.

Conscious thought was slow to return, and with it, the slick heat of his skin against mine was what I felt first. Then I was overwhelmed with all things Jackson—the weight of him pressing me into the ground, his head buried against my breasts, the soft feather-light touch of his hair tickling my chin, and our legs tangled together

His breath leveled into a whisper. It spoke to me, offering a lifetime of perfect moments like this one if I just reached out to accept it. An invitation to enter the fairy tale I'd dreamed for my happily ever after.

"That wasn't what I had in mind when we started this." He chuckled into my skin. "But fuck, that was the hottest experience of my life."

"Mmmm," I answered, too blissed out to answer in actual words.

"I've craved you every second I've known of your existence. Craved the closeness, the contact, craved the only person who has ever made me feel alive. You saved me from a life of loneliness. You can ask me for anything, and I'll do everything in my power to give it to you. You have my heart, but don't ever ask me to give you up after this. I'll tell you whatever truth you want...but I'll never tell you goodbye."

There, under that cloudless sky, surrounded by the wildflowers, I become only his in a way that the Everly of two years ago never could have.

Everything would be different now.

Or at least, that was the lie I told myself once again.

18

Unfortunately, it was time to return to my dorm after several days away. Jackson was at a special NFL prospect quarterback's camp for the weekend, so I wouldn't see him for the next few days. He'd tried to convince me to spend the weekend at his house, but I wasn't quite ready for that. Plus, Lane and I needed some girl time to catch up about everything. She'd been on a few dates with a guy from the baseball team, having sworn off her hockey lover after the Landry debacle, and I was excited to hear how it was going.

My thoughts were lost in that field with Jackson, so I wasn't paying attention to the noises coming out of my room as I grabbed on to the doorknob and swung open the door.

I wished I'd been paying attention, because opening the door and finding Caiden balls deep in Melanie was the shock of a lifetime.

I stood there aghast as I watched Caiden's perfect, tanned, toned ass thrust in and out of Melanie. Her porn star cries filled the room. I'd stumbled in on her with someone once before, but never in a thousand lifetimes would I have ever thought I'd walk in on her with Caiden.

It wasn't jealousy I was feeling, at least that confirmed once and for all that my feelings for Caiden were not like that at all.

What I was feeling was more akin to betrayal and disgust. Just a few days ago, this boy was saving me, swearing he'd look after me...and now here he was with a girl who'd done nothing but make my life hell since I'd started at this school.

Not that we'd had any deep conversations about what I suspected Melanie of doing and what I knew she'd done, but still. There had to be a code against fucking your ex-girlfriend's roommate somewhere out there.

Just like I'm sure there was a code about fucking someone's twin brother...

I continued to stand there, still as a statue, watching Caiden thrust in and out like some demented voyeur.

Suddenly Caiden's head turned, and he looked right at me, a wicked smirk on his face.

And I knew right then and there that this had been planned. For whatever reason, most likely to hurt me, Caiden had targeted Melanie, had intentionally planned this moment...wanted me to see it happen.

He held my gaze as his thrusts got faster and deeper, like looking at me was turning him on.

"Oh, Caiden," Melanie murmured throatily. Her eyes were squeezed shut in ecstasy.

I tried to get my feet to move. I tried to drag myself away from Caiden's gaze. But it was like he had me in some kind of spell. I couldn't move from my spot a step in from the doorway.

I could tell when Caiden got close because he drove into

Melanie powerfully, slamming against her until her screams of pleasure filled the air.

I had no doubt that Caiden was talented, though probably not as talented as his brother, due to his two-year hiatus and the fact that I hadn't been giving him anything the summer leading into his extended sleep, but like Jackson, Caiden's body just screamed hot sex.

I finally came to my senses and moved when Caiden's smirk grew. "Everly," he moaned as he thrust. "Everly."

My eyes widened because the bastard was imagining he was fucking me as he drove in and out of Melanie. He came with a loud groan, his gaze never leaving mine as I stumbled back into the hallway, not even caring that the door slammed shut behind me, alerting Melanie of my presence.

It took a second, but soon Melanie's angry screeching filtered out of the room. She ranted and cursed at him. I even heard a few hits. I didn't blame her. I couldn't imagine it felt great for a guy to call out another girl's name while he was inside of you. I needed to move, run away, do anything but be here, but I was frozen again in the hallway, my entire body trembling over what I'd just experienced.

That feeling in my gut, the one that had told me something was still off about Caiden, it had been right. I felt sick, disgusted...terrified. That look in his eyes. That smirk on his lips.

It was the stuff of nightmares. And I didn't need any more nightmares when it came to Caiden. I had plenty to keep me busy for the rest of my life.

But what did I do? Did I tell Jackson?

A small part of me wondered if he would believe me this time.

The door to my room opened, and Caiden sauntered out, a pleased expression on his beautifully awful face.

I swear I saw the devil in his gaze when he saw me. There was a violent energy buzzing around him as he stalked towards me.

I'd never felt more like prey than I did at this moment. I could almost see the giant fissure across Caiden's features. Like the monster inside had finally broken through and Caiden was at last manifesting who he really was.

The night of the crash, he still hadn't showed me this part of himself. Looking at him now, I could see that his actions that night had been from rage, pain...disappointment. He'd lost his mind temporarily.

But this version of Caiden, the version prowling towards me like a specter of madness, every move he made was carefully, sinisterly planned.

He pinned me against the wall before I could move. I cringed as I smelled sex and Melanie's perfume all over him. He traced his nose down my neck and then licked me savagely across my cheek. A whimper burst from my lips, and his mouth widened into an awful sneer.

"I tried to do this the nice way. I tried to get you to forgive me and see that this was all just a misunderstanding. I gave up two years of my life for my little indiscretion. It seems like you could have given me a break, you know?"

I shivered from the feeling of his breath brushing across my skin. He leaned in even closer. I steadfastly stared at the wall behind him, convinced that if I looked into his dark gaze, something bad would happen. Like I might burst into flames.

"I still remember what you taste like, LyLy," he whispered as dread curled down to my soul. "Every girl is just a stand-in until I get you back."

He backed away then and gave me a wink before he

turned and strolled down the hallway, whistling softly to himself.

My legs failed me then, and I slid down the wall, hitting the ground with a thud as I tried to hold myself together.

He'd been lying this whole time. He remembered.

§♠

I PACED IN MY ROOM. Melanie had stalked out while I was having a panic attack on the floor in the hallway. The look she'd given me was pure hate. I forced myself not to shiver at the warning shot she fired at me as she passed by.

She didn't say a word.

But she didn't need to.

I'd be sleeping with one eye open for the rest of the semester...if I slept at all.

I finally decided to text Lane, see if she wanted to have a girls' night. I needed to talk with someone about what happened, and I didn't want to distract Jackson on such an important weekend. It wasn't in any of his Rutherford files that he was bipolar, and I didn't want to risk anyone finding out by telling him something that might trigger him while he was at the camp.

Lane was all for a girls' night, and I headed out to her room as soon as she replied to my text, keeping my eyes averted from the part of the hallway where Caiden had touched me.

"Why do you look like you've seen a ghost?" Lane demanded as soon as I stepped foot in her room. Lane had two margaritas waiting and a pizza on the way. She had music blaring from her computer on her desk, a band called the Sounds of Us that we'd recently discovered.

The girl was the absolute best.

"I had a run-in with Caiden," I explained slowly, grimacing as the scene played out almost in slow-mo in my brain. "He was fucking Melanie in my room, and I walked in on them."

"Whaaat?" she shrieked. "Melanie, as in the traitorous bitch who lives with you, Melanie? And Caiden, the guy who saved you and has sworn his undying love for you, Caiden?"

I nodded. "It gets worse."

"I'm trying to think how it could get worse. Did they ask you to join in?"

Caiden's dark gaze flickered across my thoughts as he'd moved in and out of Melanie. The way he'd said my name as he came.

I shook at the memory. "I was caught off-guard, obviously, and he saw me and totally started to say my name as he orgasmed. He didn't take his eyes off me the whole time."

Lane's lips curled into a smile. "I bet Melanie loved that," she giggled.

I then proceeded to tell her about our interaction in the hallway, and her smile and laugh quickly faded.

"He's a sociopath."

I nodded, still wondering how I'd missed so many signs. I was obviously terrible at seeing who someone really was. I'd missed the signs with Landry and Professor Brady as well, which reminded me that I still needed to figure out how I was going to handle class next week with him.

But what else was I missing?

I studied Lane intently. She was in full freak-out mode, her pink-streaked hair waving agitatedly around her as she muttered something about busting a cap on Caiden's ass while she nervously bit her fingernails.

How well did I know her? Had I missed something with her as well?

I suddenly felt very much alone. I didn't want to live a life where I doubted everyone's intentions around me, but it was looking like I needed to start thinking that way.

"You're going to tell Jackson, right?" Lane asked.

I nodded. "I'm done hiding stuff from him. I just need to wait until he gets home on Sunday night. I don't want anything to mess up his training camp. This could be a huge opportunity for him."

She eyed me doubtfully. "I think he'd want to know if his psychotic twin was threatening his girlfriend."

Girlfriend. I swirled the word around in my mouth, trying to taste it and see if I liked it. This thing between Jackson and I seemed so much bigger than the words "boyfriend" or "girlfriend." After that moment in the wildflowers, the word that best seemed to fit what Jackson and I had was "forever."

And that was terrifying to me.

I wanted to tell Lane about Jackson's bipolar diagnosis right then. It would be nice to be able to have someone to talk about it with. That last episode he'd had was excruciating to think about. I had to accept that loving Jackson would always come with some very dark times. But maybe that was actually how it had to be. Jackson had to have something marring his golden perfection in order for me to fit with him. I'd always hurt beneath the scars that covered my soul. I needed someone who had damage too.

I pursed my mouth and kept my silence.

"Caiden's not going to do anything in the next two days," I told her.

"Just take him seriously this time."

I grimaced at her warning as I thought about that

summer. It had been like what I imagine a frog felt like as it was cooked to death in water turned up incrementally.

That was how that summer had been. Actions taken incrementally until it was too late.

"I know who he is now. He won't catch me off guard again," I told her, but even as the words left my mouth, I wondered if they were true. Did anyone know the real Caiden? If Jackson, who shared a womb with him, couldn't see past his mask, I wasn't sure that anyone really knew who he was.

I could taste fear in my mouth, and I hated it. Caiden was always there, even when he'd been in a coma, his influence on my life immeasurable since we'd first met.

Was there a day that I'd be able to truly escape him? I wasn't sure how it would happen. I just prayed it did.

"Okay, enough about my drama. Tell me all about your date with Brad!" I told Lane, and off she went. We spent the next hour examining every move he'd made until we determined that Brad was hopelessly in love with Lane, as he should be.

After we'd binged ourselves on junk food, bad chick flicks, and a few more margaritas, we got ready for bed. I was able to spend the night in her room, since her roommate was with her boyfriend for the night.

I hadn't heard from Jackson yet today, so I decided to text him. He'd told me that basically every hour was planned at the camp, so it was expected, but I missed him like crazy.

It was slightly pathetic.

Me: Hi.

Five minutes passed and he hadn't texted back, and Lane was snoring softly in her bed, telling me I should probably go to sleep. Heaven only knew how much sleep I would be getting when I had to go back to my room tomorrow night.

My phone buzzed.

Jackson: Hi baby.

The butterflies in my stomach began to dance at his text. We were doing this. He was calling me baby. This small thing felt big for us.

Jackson: Camp's been crazy. I threw with Tom Brady today. I might have a crush on him now too.

I had to swallow my scream. I was a big fan of all things Tom Brady, and Jackson knew it.

Jackson: Was your day good?

I hesitated, wishing he was back and I could go ahead and tell him what happened today.

Me: It was fine. Missing you.

Jackson: I have to be up at 5 for weights and conditioning. Is it ok if we talk tomorrow?

Me: Of course.

Jackson: I love you.

The butterflies in my stomach, they turned into freaking honeybees. I almost felt...happy.

Me: Love you too.

I plugged in my phone to my charger and then read his text over and over again until I fell asleep.

&

MELANIE WAS BLISSFULLY absent when I returned to my room the next evening. Lane had just left for a date with Brad after we'd spent hours getting her ready, and she'd told me just to stay in her room and wait for her. But her roommate was back, and the girl was not fond of me for whatever reason. So I was back in my dorm again, flinching at every sound, thinking it meant Melanie was about to walk in.

After exchanging a few more texts with Jackson, who had another early morning the next day, I changed into some lounging clothes, deciding that I would just read in bed for the rest of the night and then sleep in Lane's room tomorrow during the day.

I didn't care if Jackson had to use his popularity with the front office, I was switching rooms next week.

I started reading a book, chugging an energy drink to try and stay awake.

But I must have fallen asleep anyway.

I was awakened by searing pain in my scalp as Melanie dragged me by my hair off my bed. "You fucking bitch," she seethed as she knocked my head against my desk while pulling me to the ground.

I thrashed against her, panic scratching at my spine when I realized that the psycho had managed to tie my hands together while I was sleeping.

I must have been more tired than I thought.

"What the fuck is wrong with you?" I yelled as I tried to get my hair out of her grip. With how hard she was pulling, I was pretty sure I was in danger of being scalped at any moment.

I looked up at her as I continued to struggle. Melanie was makeup-less, her hair up in a ponytail, a crazed look in her gaze as she stared down at me, holding onto me tightly.

"You've ruined everything. He would've been mine if you'd never showed up, ya know? He was mine that summer, spending every night in my bed after he finished with you." She rambled on and on, and it took me a second to figure out what she was talking about. Or should I say, who...

"Are you talking about Caiden?" I groaned, confused, as she slammed my head against the ground for good measure.

"Of course I'm talking about Caiden, you idiot. He was mine. He was my boyfriend in high school. He loved me. And then you lured him away with your little sob story. And he felt sorry for you, so he spent time with you, acted like your boyfriend because you begged him to. But he wanted to be with me. Every second he could get away from you, he was with me." Angry tears fell down her face as she spoke, not even realizing that with her words, she'd once again reshaped a summer that I'd just thought I'd finally figured out.

"You knew him in high school?" I asked dumbly, facts failing to connect because I was pretty sure I'd just sustained another concussion, which couldn't be good since I'd just recovered from one.

"You really haven't been able to recognize me." She laughed.

They told you the key was to keep an assailant talking until you could get help. But in this case, I really was interested in everything that she was saying. I just was having trouble comprehending it.

"I went to Northridge High. I bet I was at almost all of the parties you were at."

She didn't look familiar to me at all.

"It figures," she spat out, obviously having read the lack of recognition on my face. "Everly James doesn't care about anyone but herself."

She began to hum to herself, as if she was lost in another world, before she shook her head and refocused...on me.

"Caiden talked about you all the time. About how you were stringing Jackson along, about how selfish you were.

You ruined his life. You and your magic pussy that you wouldn't give him."

She put her knee in my stomach as she leaned over to get something, still keeping a firm grip on my hair with her other hand.

My eyes watered as the pressure on my gut and skull intensified.

I began to struggle again when I saw what she'd grabbed.

It was a knife.

"You've just got him confused right now. He's just feeling sorry for you," she muttered practically to herself as she stared at the knife, fascinated. "He didn't mean to say your name. He didn't mean it."

She shot me a piercing glare. "I've done everything to get rid of you. He told me about your fear of the dark back in high school. Have you liked my little games? Pushing you down the stairs wasn't really part of the plan, but I couldn't resist it when I saw you up there." She grinned wildly.

"You're insane," I told her through gritted teeth as I tried to control my urge to cry from the pain. At least now I knew who'd been behind everything. That fucking snake. "You can't think that whatever plan you have in your head is going to work."

"He's just too nice. He can't get rid of you. But if I do it, he'll help me. I know he will. Because he loves me." Her voice came out in a sing-song, high-pitched tone that couldn't have gotten any creepier.

My shock at the rude awakening and the craziness that she spewed finally faded, replaced by outright terror as I realized that she'd truly lost it. It wasn't out of the realm of possibility for her to try and kill me with how she sounded and looked right now.

"Melanie, Caiden does this. He manipulates people. Has he actually told you he loved you?" I tried to plead to whatever reason was left in her brain. Whatever Caiden had done to this girl, I knew it had nothing to do with love.

At this point, I didn't think that he was capable of such a feeling.

"He loves me. I know he does," she told me frantically, and a wave of pity hit me, even amidst the fear, because she really believed it even though he hadn't said it.

She suddenly dropped the knife and grinned down at me, even as I struggled against her. My head felt like it was loaded with concrete, so my movements felt stiff and uncoordinated. My poor brain.

"I think I want to make this as personal as possible," she whispered manically as she let go of my hair and laid both hands around my throat, beginning to press harder and harder, until I couldn't breathe at all and it felt like she was going to crush my windpipe.

This crazy bitch really was about to kill me.

I struggled as hard as I could, but she was persistent, continuing to squeeze with all her might. The world started to fade, the literal light at the end of the tunnel of my vision getting smaller and smaller, until I knew it was the end.

I suddenly heard a loud crash and then what sounded like a war cry. Melanie screeched above me as her hands suddenly loosened and her body flopped off of me, letting in a gulp of beautiful, beautiful air.

Lane's panicked face appeared in front of my hazy vision, and then I felt hands pulling on the ropes around my wrists. A few seconds later, my hands were free, but all I could do was lay there and try to get my breath back.

I heard Lane screaming at someone, and I faintly realized that she must have called the police.

Her face popped into my view again. "Everly, please say something. The police are on their way." Tears dripped on my face as she continued to hover right above me.

"Melanie?" I finally asked in a scratchy voice.

"I knocked that bitch out. She might be dead. But I don't care. I'll pray later," Lane said fiercely.

She helped me up after a few more minutes when I regained some of my strength, and we huddled together across from Melanie's still, prone form on the floor next to us.

We heard loud stomping down the hallway a minute later, and then five police officers ran into the room. They took one look at Melanie's body and turned their attention to us.

Lane held up her hands. "I was the one who called you. She was about to kill my friend," she shouted.

The police hesitated for a moment, and Melanie chose that moment to let out a loud groan, obviously not dead. Thank goodness...

Her eyes flew open, and somehow, the psycho managed to lunge at me, despite the gaping head wound she had from where Lane had hit her.

The police grabbed her before she could get something, and she thrashed in their arms, screaming obscenities at me.

That cleared it up pretty well for the police as to what exactly had happened.

An ambulance came, and the responders confirmed that I most likely had a concussion and a bruised trachea. Since I knew there was really nothing they could do for me, I had them leave.

I didn't think that Melanie would be returning to

Rutherford any time soon...if ever. Which meant that I had my room to myself to recover.

Thank fuck.

The door finally closed as the last police officer left after taking our statement.

Lane and I sat there on my bed, not saying a word.

I fiddled with my collarbone absentmindedly, still trying to catch up with what had just happened.

Melanie had tried to kill me.

Caiden had been sleeping with Melanie the whole summer he was with me.

Melanie had tried to kill me.

I absorbed the sentences, letting them settle in until I could accept them as truth.

I hated that it was still my first reaction to deny that Caiden could do something.

By now it was obvious Caiden could do anything. And he had done everything.

I turned to look at Lane, who was staring blankly at the wall, shaking slightly as she came down from the adrenaline rush, I assumed.

"You saved me," I whispered, tears of gratitude laced through my words.

Lane finally turned to stare at me. And then she burst into tears. Snotty, messy tears. She buried her head in my shoulder, and I softly stroked her hair and tried to comfort her, even though my head and my throat were killing me.

"You've got to stop almost dying on me," she sniffed after a minute, pulling her head off my shoulder and looking at me with a watery gaze. "I'm going to have to start taking karate or get a weapons' permit if this keeps up, and my mother will not be happy with me, since she's firmly against violence."

"We wouldn't want that," I told her with a small grin.

"You're my best friend. You've got to stay alive," she told me insistently, like I had a choice in all of this.

I nodded again, thinking how tired I was.

And how the fuck was I going to explain all of this to Jackson tomorrow evening when he came home?

Lane dragged her bedding from downstairs, saying that she was going to spend the night and make sure I didn't die. We stripped off Melanie's bedding, and then Lane unceremoniously dumped it out the window, both of us watching as the sheets fluttered to the ground.

Looking at the sheets just reminded me of her and Caiden, and I grimaced and pulled away, crawling into my bed wearily.

Lane got into her bed and we said goodnight, even though by this point, it was three in the morning.

I was exhausted, my brain ready to call it quits, but I kept thinking of Melanie's story and the fact that Caiden was out there somewhere on campus.

And I just knew he was biding his time.

19

I opened the door, and there he was. Sometimes, I didn't know if I dreamed Jackson up or not. And then he would appear, and I'd wonder how something so beautiful could ever belong to me. It seemed like it was just yesterday that I was furious at him, and now somehow, he'd succeeded in making his arms feel like home to me. I was enthralled with the sense of bliss I found myself in, even though the real world...and Caiden waited just behind him.

"I've been thinking the whole ride home about our first kiss," he told me with no preamble as he stepped into my room. Lane had left a few hours earlier to catch up on some school work with Brad, so it was just him and me.

"Excuse me?" I asked, thoroughly confused.

"The first kiss we should have had. The one that was stolen from us."

"Oh," I said, disappointed at just the mention of my kiss with Caiden.

"I thought we could have a redo. We could have a new first kiss, one that we always could go back to. We could replace those other kisses with a kiss like it should have been."

I eyed him doubtfully. He looked so hopeful though, standing there in the fading light from the window in the hallway hitting his hair just perfectly, gilding his features, turning him into the angel I'd begun to imagine he was again.

I nodded, because I didn't know if I could say no to him about anything anymore.

He cupped my chin. With the lightest of pressure, he tilted my head gently back and slowly lowered his face closer to mine. "This should have been your first kiss, Everly."

My belly filled with fire, and my cheeks flushed with heat. I could barely breathe from his whispered words. As if a breeze, his warm lips brushed against mine. Jackson's hand trailed feather-soft fingers down my neck, making my skin tingle with what felt like flames. The outside sounds of the activity in the rest of the dorm grew faint, and all I could hear was our quick, shallow breaths as his mouth moved against mine. Heat traveled down my neck and across my chest, tightening my skin and coiling my muscles. I never knew such a feeling existed in such a simple touch of lips.

"What the fuck is this?" Jackson growled suddenly, breaking the spell he'd cast around us.

The fingerprints. Right. The concussion. Right.

"It's been an eventful weekend," I told him.

Jackson was trembling, still eyeing the marks on my neck.

"I need you to stay with me when I tell you what happened," I begged. "I need you here with me."

Jackson shook his head violently. I didn't think it was

possible for him to control his episodes, but I was wishing on a thousand stars right then that it was.

"What the fuck happened, Everly?"

I told him everything then, leaving nothing out. Jackson let out a string of curses when I told him about Caiden and Melanie and then our interaction in the hallway. But he really went crazy after he heard what happened with Melanie the night before.

"Why didn't you call me, text me, call the emergency contact number for the camp?" he roared, the loud noise sending pangs through my fragile head.

"I didn't want to distract you. This weekend was important," I told him, annoyed with his tone.

He pulled me towards him, his fingertips dancing over my bruises softly. "When are you going to get through your pretty head that you are the most important thing to me? I've lived without you. I know that there isn't anything in this world that deserves to take precedence over you."

They were pretty words, but a part of me still doubted.

"I took your brother away from you," I blurted out.

He raised an eyebrow.

"I took your brother away from you, and I'm never going to take anything else from you again."

"Baby, you didn't take anything away from me. You don't owe me anything. I'm the one who owes you. Please, promise me that you'll call me, no matter what. I want to know if something falls in the middle of the night and scares you, I want to know when you hit your funny bone, I want to know every inane detail about your life. I need you to trust that I can be there for you, no matter what."

Jackson gazed at me with those blue eyes that looked like they'd been touched by storm clouds today. I lost my breath for a second at the love I saw in their depths.

"How can you look at me like that?"

"Like what?"

"Like I'm everything."

He smiled slightly. "Oh baby, it's easy. You're the most beautiful thing I've ever known. I can't look at you any other way."

Jackson loved me.

The irrefutable truth of the statement sparked my heart, creating an impenetrable barrier of strength in my soul that told me I could do anything as long as he was with me.

Jackson sat on my bed, pulling me into his arms. I nuzzled my face in the crook of his neck as we sat there and absorbed the silence.

Finally, I pulled away.

"What are we going to do about Caiden?" I asked.

A look of determination took shape on Jackson's face.

"I'll deal with Caiden."

I wished in that moment that it would be that simple. That Jackson could stop Caiden on his own.

I had a feeling it wouldn't be that easy.

"Let's go get something to eat, and we can figure out what to do. I think the first step is you moving to my place."

I shifted uncomfortably. Moving in with him seemed like a really huge step. "I'll be alone in this room from now on, I assume."

"Can you honestly say you'll feel comfortable sleeping in here alone? I mean, if you want me to start sleeping in here every night, that's fine, but we're going to need to order a new bed."

I scoffed, thinking of Jackson moving in here when he had his shiny, new townhome.

"We'll talk about it later," I told him. "I'm starving."

Jackson looked confident he would get his way, but he

let me lead him out of the room and then to my favorite pizza place down the street from the academy, where I drowned my sorrows in greasy carbs.

"We should have grabbed the rocky road ice cream too," Jackson complained as I got out my key to unlock my dorm room door.

I put the key in the lock...and quickly realized that the door was unlocked.

And I knew I'd locked it on my way out. My hand trembled as I clenched the key tightly.

"What's wrong?" asked Jackson.

"The door's unlocked," I whispered, my words choking on my rising fear.

A grim look crossed Jackson's face, and he pushed me gently behind him as he slowly opened the door and flipped on the light.

"Fuck," he snarled.

I peeked my head into the room before he could stop me from coming in, and I cried out when I saw the ripped apart carcass of an enormous snake all over my bed. The snake's red blood was splattered all over my bedspread and the wall behind my bed.

I plastered my hand to my mouth, trying to quell the urge to be sick.

"What's with the snakes?" I moaned.

"We both knew you were scared of them," Jackson absentmindedly responded, looking at a torn-out piece of paper that had been placed next to the blood and guts of the snake.

My gaze snapped to him. "You were responsible for the snake in my shower?" I gasped in horror. "I thought that was one of the things Melanie did."

Jackson had the decency to blush as he brushed a hand

through his hair, embarrassed. "I have immunity now, right? You're not going to run away from me?"

I scrunched up my nose in disgust. "What else did you do? What about the night from hell in the storage shed?"

Jackson shook his head vigorously in denial. "I didn't have time to do anything else before we started having sex. And I wouldn't do something like that to you. Even as messed up as I was over you, I wouldn't have gone that far."

I huffed. "The snake was going too far." My gaze flicked to the destroyed snake tarnishing my room.

I shivered.

"I'm sorry, little angel," Jackson whispered as he came up to me and enveloped me in his arms.

"What did that note say?" I asked, ignoring his apology and vowing to get back at him someday. Maybe a spider. Jackson was terrified of spiders.

"I'll deal with it," he answered vaguely.

"Just let me see it," I snapped.

Jackson reluctantly handed the piece of notebook paper to me.

For You LyLy, was all it said, in Caiden's bold handwriting.

But it was enough to stoke the embers of fear inside of me that Caiden's existence always kept present.

He was coming for me. I was never going to get away from him.

"You're moving to my place," Jackson said firmly.

I didn't argue this time.

20

Jackson

I was done playing nice. Caiden obviously wanted to play dirty, and I could do dirty with the best of them. Especially after hearing Everly scream in the middle of the night as she came out of a nightmare starring Caiden.

I went hunting for Caiden the next morning. I stopped at his dorm first, but my teammates who lived there said they hadn't seen him in a few days. It was the same for everyone else on campus that would have any clue where he was.

Caiden had disappeared.

On a whim, I called my parents.

"What do you need Jackson?" my dad answered, annoyed.

"Hello to you too, Dad."

"Your mother and I are very disappointed. Your brother is here, and he's told us all about your behavior at the school. Sleeping with Caiden's girlfriend, harassing Everly. I'm regretting the day you were ever born!"

C.R. JANE

It took me a second to respond, because I was so fucking shocked at the words that had just come out of my father's asshole...I mean mouth.

"You've got to be shitting me," I finally said, in what I was proud was a calm voice.

"We've had to cover up a lot of your fuck-ups, Jackson. But enough is enough. This is too far. We're cutting you off."

I pinched the bridge of my nose, trying to stay calm. The last thing I needed was to go black right now. Everly would be left all alone.

Please, God. Don't let me go black.

"He's lying about everything. He beat Everly half to death the night of the accident, and he's been basically stalking her since he woke up," I tried to explain to him.

"Why on earth would Caiden be stalking that trash?"

I wished I could reach through the phone and land a fist in my father's stupid fucking face at that moment.

"He's obsessed? I don't know...you would have to ask him why he's such a psychopath."

"Jackson, you've been jealous of your brother since almost the moment you were born. I'm not going to listen to this crap for one more minute."

I heard Caiden's smug voice in the background, and then the line went dead. He'd hung up on me.

Well, at least I knew where Caiden was. The snake had returned to his hole.

I went to the administration the following morning with Everly and reported Caiden.

The school dean had a flabbergasted look on his face as we laid out all of Caiden's sins, his mouth opening and closing in shock.

When we'd finished outlining everything, there was a long pause.

Heartbreak Lover

"Are you sure it was Caiden?" the dean finally said, and I shot him a disgusted look.

"I'm positive. So do your job."

"Have you spoken to your parents about this?" I scoffed, knowing he was worried about losing the sizeable donation that my parents provided to the school every year.

"Let's just say that my parent's donation will be the least of your concerns if Caiden is still a student here by the end of the day."

Dean Lewis puffed up like a peacock, his enormous stomach threatening to bust his shirt open as he poked his chest out, trying to look intimidating.

"Are you threatening me, Mr. Parker?" he asked in a tight voice.

"Of course not. I'm simply saying that if he's still in the school, this story will be everywhere. I'm sure that your other donors will have a lot of questions as to why such a fine institution as Rutherford Academy would be allowing such acts to happen in its hallowed halls."

Dean Lewis stared at me, a tic moving rapidly in his left cheek. He hated me.

And there was nothing he could do about it.

"I'll see what I can do," he finally seethed.

"Do better than that," I warned as I dragged Everly out of the office behind me.

"This is going to send him over the edge, don't you think?" Everly asked, worriedly.

It would, but that was what I was counting on.

"Either that, or he'll give up."

Everly nodded, but I knew she didn't believe that he would give up.

I didn't believe it either.

Caiden had been texting her constantly since about an

hour after we'd discovered the snake. No matter how many times she blocked his number, he'd text her from another number, until finally, she'd just turned off her phone.

The texts had terrified her, a strange mix of threats and obscene descriptions of all his sexual fantasies he had concerning her. We'd saved all of them in case we needed to get her a restraining order, but I was worried it wouldn't be enough, or that a restraining order wouldn't do a damn thing in the first place.

I might've been able to put pressure on Rutherford Academy, thanks to my position as the number one quarterback in the country, but my parents held all the power outside of these walls. They could make a restraining order disappear in a flash, if it meant protecting their beloved son.

My heart clenched, thinking of this latest betrayal.

I'm regretting the day you were ever born.

My father's words shouldn't have stung so badly. I'd been hearing a version of them ever since my diagnosis.

But somehow, they still hurt.

Everly's warm, lithe body pressed against me just then, and the pain quieted.

As long as I had her, nothing else mattered.

Please, God. Don't let me go black.

Everly

The shrill whaling of the fire alarm jolted us both awake. I inhaled in surprise at the rude awakening and immediately began coughing as smoke filled my lungs. Tears washed over my eyes.

The entire room was cast in a hazy cloud of dark smoke that had fear sparking up my limbs.

"Shit. We have to get out of here," Jackson yelled, panicked.

He hastily pulled on his pants and threw me my sleep shorts and tank top that he'd ripped off earlier when he'd devoured me before falling asleep.

"Hurry," he urged me as he ran to the door and tapped the doorknob carefully, checking to see if it was hot.

"It's still cool."

Jackson wrapped his arm around my waist and led me down the hallway and down the stairs.

We turned the corner and stopped when we saw that the kitchen was entirely engulfed in flames. The whole house smelled of gas, and I dimly realized that all of the burners on the stove were on, pouring gas into the air.

"We have to get out of here," I cried, and Jackson yanked me back the way we came, towards the small office on the opposite side of the first floor.

He yanked open a window, and we crawled out, coughing and choking on the thick smoke that followed us out the window.

Jackson swept me up in his arms and carried me across the street. We could hear sirens in the distance, assumedly coming here, but they would get here too late. There was an explosion just then, like something out of a horror movie. Right before our eyes, the house became nothing but twisted plastic and charred wood, acrid smoke pouring into the night air.

Two fire trucks came racing onto the street, and my attention got caught on a familiar silver Range Rover that was parked at the end of the street.

As if pulled by a string, I took a step forward, my gaze straining to look at the figure sitting in the car.

Caiden's face appeared in the window as he leaned his head out the driver's window and blew me a kiss.

I backed away quickly, as if I was in danger of him reaching out and grabbing me, even from that far away.

"Jackson," I whispered, trembling as I grabbed onto his sleeve. Jackson looked over and saw Caiden as he pulled away, Caiden gifting him with a wave.

Caiden was playing on a whole other level.

I didn't know if we could keep up.

JACKSON and I wearily walked into the hotel room that he'd rented for us to stay for the night. His first credit card had been declined, his parent's fulfilling their promise to cut him off. I was tired all the way to my bones...I was tired to my soul.

Caiden had sent a video to Jackson's phone, obviously meant for me, of him jacking off into a pair of underwear that I clearly recognized as mine.

The police had made the night even better by telling us they had no way of proving Caiden had started the fire, due to the alibi his parents had given him and the condition of Jackson's destroyed house.

To say we were stressed was an understatement for how we were feeling.

We showered the ash and smoke off in the shower, our hands trailing along each other's skin in an effort to provide comfort.

I slid into bed, and Jackson collapsed next to me, his hand across his eyes.

Fear flickered as I tried to get a glimpse of his eyes.

Sometimes, I forgot that he was a time bomb, and it was stressful events just like this that could trigger him.

He slid his hand off his face, and I sighed in relief as I got a glimpse of his cool, blue eyes. He was still with me. I wouldn't have to be alone.

At least for now.

"Stay with me," I pleaded to him when he looked at me questioningly.

Understanding filled his gaze. "Always," he murmured, and even though I knew it was a promise that he couldn't keep...I welcomed his answering kiss. So gentle, even when I tried to deepen it, he forced the pace, and it was slow, tender. Moving his body over me, he worshipped every inch of my body, with his mouth and tongue, hands and fingers, then finally, his body. Hard yet soft at the same time, he took me with a soothing glide, yet I screamed his name as I crashed around him. Tears streaked down the sides of my face and into my hair. I loved him. Forever and ever. No matter what happened, his kiss...his touch...him, he was all that mattered.

I listened to Jackson's deep breaths in the dark, and my thoughts drifted to Caiden.

A tear slid down my face as I went through everything he had done.

I could now see all of Caiden's demons, and it was truly the tragedy of a lifetime that they all looked like me.

21

"I have to take that exam," I told Jackson as I worried my lip. "And you have to go to that meeting with your coach."

"I'll skip it," he said nonchalantly, even though I knew how important the meeting was.

"I'll take the exam, and then Lane will walk with me to your practice. We've already mapped out our route."

"No," he said firmly.

"Jackson, I have to take that test. The professor already said he'd fail me if I didn't show up. I missed five of his classes this semester, and he only allows one absence. I can't afford to lose my scholarship."

"I'll bribe someone."

I glared at him, and he groaned.

"The exam and that's it," he demanded.

I nodded, relieved that he'd agreed. I hadn't told him that I was in danger of losing my scholarship, even if I took this exam. Everything that happened this semester hadn't exactly been helpful in my academic life. And I didn't want him to worry anymore about me.

An hour later, we parted ways. Jackson dropped me off at my class, not leaving the entryway until I'd sat down in my seat. The professor shot us both an exasperated look, and I was sure he thought that we were pathetic, love-struck teenagers that dramatically didn't want to be parted.

If he only knew.

We started the test. I was exhausted from a sleepless night spent worrying, and I hadn't spent nearly enough time studying...so it wasn't going well.

The door opened, and I looked up as an administrative aid walked in and handed Professor Charles a note before leaving the room.

He frowned as he read it, and then he looked up, his gaze finding mine.

"Ms. James, please come here."

I stood up shakily and walked to the front of the room. "You've been summoned to the dean's office," he said exasperatedly. "You'd better get going. I expect you back afterwards to finish your exam, no matter what else you have planned today or how late it is."

"I'll just go after," I told him pleadingly, but he rolled his eyes and shook his head.

"Just go, Ms. James, before you cause any more disturbances. I know you couldn't care less about this class, based on your dismal attendance record, but I'll not have you messing up exams for the students that do care."

I heard students tittering behind me, and my cheeks flushed. If he only knew how much I did care.

I gave up and walked stiffly out the door, not looking at anyone.

I'd just stepped outside when I realized that I'd forgotten my phone by my desk, obviously not knowing that I was going to be forced to leave when I'd been called up to talk to the professor.

I poked my head back into the classroom to grab my phone.

"Why are you still here, Ms. James?" the professor asked snidely.

"I just need to grab—"

"Get to the office now," he ordered.

I nodded weakly.

Telling myself everything would be fine, I took off for the dean's office, hating how quiet the halls were with everyone in class.

I'd just stepped through the back doors of the English building, when a pair of hands grabbed me and a wet cloth was placed over my nose.

I struggled for a second before collapsing in my captor's arms. My last image was of a red-haired girl peering out from the window by the door, a terrified look on her face.

❧

A HAND STROKED my face softly, and I leaned into the warm touch, moaning softly.

"Wake up, Everly," Caiden's voice called out gently. "Wake up."

Why was Caiden telling me to wake up? I was in bed with Jackson. I didn't want to wake up.

"So tired," I mumbled.

"Wake up," Caiden repeated again.

My eyes cracked open, and I looked up from where I was lying to see Caiden hovering above my face, a euphoric look on his features.

"There's my beautiful girl."

Heartbreak Lover

I stared up at him, completely out of sorts, wondering why Caiden was here with me.

It took me a minute, and then everything rushed to focus. I had been called to the dean's office, a pair of hands had grabbed me.

Caiden.

I began to struggle frantically. I was in a house that I didn't recognize with Caiden, my legs tied together.

This was the stuff that nightmares were made of.

Caiden's lips curled up in annoyance. "Stop struggling. You're not going anywhere."

I reared up, knocking my head against Caiden's nose, and he cursed as he pulled away from me, holding his nose.

I rolled over and began to army crawl across the floor as best I could away from him, knowing that I wouldn't get far but making the effort anyway.

I made it halfway across the polished wood floor before Caiden was on me, picking me up and tossing me on the gray leather couch pushed against one of the walls. I immediately started to struggle again, until Caiden slapped his hand harshly on the coffee table in front of the couch.

"I'm not going to hit you," Caiden said calmly, the anger he was hiding displayed in the tick in his cheek. "You're expecting me to hit you, and I'm showing you that I've changed so you'll finally forgive me and we can be together."

I stopped my useless movements and stared at him in shock. His eyes were slightly out of focus, and there was a flush to his cheeks.

"We can't be together, Caiden," I told him, even though I knew it would just make him mad.

"You keep saying that," Caiden said with a chuckle. "You just needed to get away from Jackson. He's been controlling you, warping your mind. You're forgetting how good we were together."

Oh, Caiden.

I decided to try and reason with him. "Caiden, you were sleeping with Melanie the whole time we were dating. We weren't good together. I wasn't giving you what you needed."

"You're the only thing I need," he snapped harshly before taking a deep breath and pushing a hand through his hair as he struggled to control his temper. "Melanie didn't mean anything. I just needed an outlet because I didn't want to push you to do something you weren't ready for. I was being a good boyfriend. I couldn't care fucking less about Melanie. *You* are the only thing I care about." His voice was emphatic, like he was desperate for me to believe him.

"What about your brother?" I pleaded with him. "You can't keep this up. Don't you care at all about him?"

"I don't want to hear you talk about him, do you understand me?" he snarled, and I pushed back against the couch, fear snaking through my insides.

All right...talking about Jackson was not the right approach in this situation.

Caiden pulled a gun out from a bag on the coffee table and then sat in an armchair across from me and began to polish it, whistling that same tune that I'd heard him hum at my dorm. It was the perfect soundtrack for a madman. I tracked the gun as he moved it around, terror clenching at my throat.

"What are you going to do with me?" I asked quietly, giving up trying to get away for the moment.

"I once read about Stockholm syndrome. It's a real thing, evidently. If I keep you with me long enough, you'll fall back in love with me. You were in love with me once, you can be in love with me again." He said all of this in a mild, reasonable voice that didn't fit with the craziness he was spewing.

I shook at his words, tears beginning to stream down my face.

"Caiden, please. Don't do this. Just think about what you're doing," I begged him, searching his face for some kind of sanity.

"I have thought about this. I've thought about this since the moment I met you when we were just kids. I thought about how much I loved you. How good our lives would be together." He shook his head as if the memories were too much, clenching his teeth together like he was in agony.

He stood up, set the gun down, and pulled a small box from his pocket. My heart thudded out of my chest as I watched him open it up, revealing a beautiful diamond ring. He held it out to me, a cruel offering of a desperate love that I never wanted.

"I bought this that summer. I thought maybe it could be a promise ring until we were older. I carried it around with me everywhere, waiting for the right moment. And then you fucking broke up with me."

He stared at me desperately. "I love you, Everly James. I love you more than life itself. Everything I've done, I've done for us. Why can't you just love me back?"

Love. What a strange concept. The greatest sins of humanity had been done in the name of love, yet we all craved it, were desperate for it. Myself included.

Caiden's version of love had become so disfigured that I didn't know what you could call it anymore.

Eyeing the gun that he'd set down on his armchair, cold realization filled me.

Caiden was going to kill me because of that love.

. . .

Jackson

My knee bounced anxiously as I listened to my coach and my agent talk about the NFL scouts that had inquired about me. Coach wanted to know how many years he was going to have me, and Tom, my douche bag agent, wanted to know when he could start making money off of me.

I wanted them both to fuck themselves.

I'd lived and breathed football my whole life, but right now...I couldn't have cared less about anything to do with it.

My heart and mind were with a green-eyed beauty taking her English literature exam. I wondered how mad she would get if I appeared in her class before it was over. I was supposed to go to practice after this, but fuck that. Until this thing with my sociopath of a brother was figured out, everything else but Everly would have to wait.

A fist beat on the door just then, and Kyle popped his head in before Coach could tell him to come in.

"Jackson, I need to talk to you. *Now*," he told me anxiously.

"Kyle, we're in a meeting right now—" Coach tried to say, but I was already out of my seat and jogging towards Kyle. There were only two reasons why he would come find me right now since he knew I was in this meeting—Caiden or Everly.

"Parker," Coach called after me, but I was already in the hallway, the office door closing behind me, not bothering to explain myself.

"Kasey saw Caiden take Everly," Kyle said with no preamble. "She was in the English building, about to walk outside, when Caiden grabbed Everly and put some kind of cloth on her face that made her pass out. She ran and told a professor, but he didn't seem too concerned. She called me because I'd told her you and Everly were together, and I had her call the police, but fuck man, this is bad."

She was gone. The thought crippled my brain, even when I should've been absorbed in getting as much information about what Kasey, Kyle's girlfriend, saw. Bile rose, burning my esophagus with the truth.

Caiden had her.

There was an aching emptiness in my heart. Tentacles of fear strangled the life out of me one breath at a time. I had never known its full strength before now, not even after the accident. Every memory with Everly became a blurred slide clicking into place, the vibrancy bled dry in comparison to the bright terror of this moment. I was paralyzed by my failure to protect her.

"Jackson, stay with me," I faintly heard Kyle say frantically. Kyle knew about my bipolar, he knew that I would be worthless in helping Everly if I fell into an episode. I could feel it creeping in, and I began to take deep breaths, trying to get ahold of myself. I couldn't control it, but I'd do everything I could to try.

Kyle put a hand to my shoulder. I hung my head, running a hand along the headache forming beneath it.

"Do you have any idea where he would have taken her?" Kyle asked.

I shook my head, shrugging his hand off and beginning to jog down the hallway and through the exit so I could get to my truck.

"You said the police were called?" I yelled out behind me.

"Yeah, but I don't know if they're taking it seriously or not."

I swore, just betting they weren't. As soon as Kasey had

mentioned Caiden's name, they'd probably stopped listening.

Fucking Caiden. I would kill him with my bare hands when I got ahold of him.

The fear came back, replacing the anger. Terror surfaced in my ragged pulse because I was afraid no matter how hard I looked, she wouldn't come back to me. Caiden's mind was so far beyond my comprehension at this point, I felt helpless to stop him.

Just then my phone in my pocket buzzed. I pulled it out, hoping it was something about Everly.

It was. Caiden had texted me.

Everly was sitting on a gray leather couch, her eyes a dark void as she stared at the camera. I could see that he'd bound her legs together.

Caiden had accompanied the picture with, *My girlfriend sends her best.*

Not thinking, I responded with *Fuck you* before throwing my phone in the passenger seat of my truck and beating my hands against my steering wheel in a fury.

Once I'd gotten at least a little ahold of myself, I grabbed my phone and turned on my truck, driving around desperately while I called as many people as possible, begging them if they knew anything about where Caiden would be.

Hours passed, and no one had seen him. I'd called the police station, and they'd asked if it had been twenty-four hours since Everly had disappeared. Fucking idiots.

Not knowing what to do, I called my parents.

"I knew you'd come crawling back after we canceled your credit cards," my father coldly remarked when he answered the phone.

My mind raced as I debated exactly how to play this.

Heartbreak Lover

"You were right. I was out of control. I need help," I told him.

A pleased hum came through the phone.

"I was hoping that I could start fixing things with Caiden first, and then I'll come home, and we can go to the doctor," I told him, every word tasting like acid in my mouth. I kept my words as innocent as possible, trying to channel my twin's unparalleled manipulation tactics. "Do you know where he is?"

"Probably at his new place," my father said in a pleased voice. The bastard was over the moon at my mea culpa.

"New place?" My heart clenched with this new information.

"You have a lot to work out with your brother if he didn't tell you we got him a townhome, just down the street from yours. I would have liked you two to be able to live together, but we didn't want your out of control behavior to stunt his recovery."

"Of course," I said, struggling to keep my voice mild, even though I was literally shaking as I did an illegal U-turn and raced towards my former residence.

"What's the unit number? I want to stop by right now and say sorry."

My father rattled off the number, and I thanked him profusely, promising that I would be right over as soon as I talked to Caiden.

Setting the phone down after we'd disconnected, I tried to control my shaking. It was a bit ironic that my father had unwittingly aided me in saving Everly. If he'd known my real intentions for needing Caiden's address, he would have never given me the information.

Fucking bastard, I seethed, vowing that after this, I would never speak to my parents again.

I sent up a silent prayer to a god that had forgotten me long ago that Caiden had taken Everly to his new place.

I drove up to the unit next to his, dimming the headlights as I parked. A spark of hope lit up inside of me when I saw that the lights inside of Caiden's place were on.

I killed the engine and texted Kyle the address, telling him to call the police if I didn't text him in ten minutes.

And then I got out the bat that I kept under the backseat of the truck and strode towards his place.

I peered through the front windows, trying to see any sign of Everly or Caiden. A shadow finally moved in the hallway, and I slipped out of sight when Caiden appeared, striding down the hall.

She had to be here.

I jogged to the back of the house, opposite of the direction Caiden had been headed, and I took out my pocketknife and began to fiddle with one of the larger windows.

Caiden and I had become pretty adept at breaking and entering early on in middle school, after our parents had tried to keep us in the house and away from Everly.

It had been awhile since I needed the skill, so it took a few minutes to pick the lock on the window.

I silently celebrated when a soft click sounded, signaling that I'd finally gotten it unlocked.

Here I come, little angel.

22

Everly

I was wearing the fucking ring. Caiden had placed it on my finger, giving my ring finger a soft kiss as he'd done so. I was in shock, so I didn't put up a fight.

And now I was wearing his fucking ring, trapped in what seemed like another dimension where up was down and crazy was sane.

"You look so beautiful, LyLy. Our wedding night is going to be so perfect."

"Wedding night?" I whispered, and I watched in horror as his eyes lit up.

"Of course. As soon as possible," he assured me proudly.

Fuck no. This had gone on long enough. I was tired and afraid. And really fucking tired of being tired and afraid.

I was fast for once, too fast for him to respond. My thumb scraped his nose and then gouged at his eye. He screamed, and I reveled in the sound, jumping up from the couch and aiming an elbow at the back of his bent over head.

With my legs together, all I could do was hop across the floor, but I did it, going as fast as I could like I was in the Olympics.

I'd almost made it out of the room when Caiden tackled me, sending sharp pain to every limb as we crashed to the floor. I struggled against him, my cheek scraping against the tile as he muttered curses at me.

"I didn't want to do this, Everly. I hated doing it at the club. I hated watching Landry put his disgusting hands on you. But it was necessary then. Just like this will be necessary now. If I have to fuck you into submission, I will."

My god, Caiden had been the one to drug me on Lane's birthday. The depths of his manipulative darkness were so deep that I didn't think it was possible to find the bottom of it.

Caiden had begun to pull at my clothes, and I started to cry as I tried to struggle under him to no avail.

I was praying for death when I heard a loud crack, and Caiden went limp on top of me.

I stilled, trembling, wondering what other monster was now in the room.

Caiden was rolled off of me with a thud, and then I was flipped over.

A cry of relief burst from my lips when I saw who it was.

It was my monster that was there, looking down at me in relief.

Jackson had come.

Jackson quickly untied me and gathered me in his arms. His touch was feather-light, yet fierce at the same time. I buried myself in my favorite place in that space between his head and shoulder and clung to him, hands in his hair, lips to his thundering pulse. I sank in as close as humanly possible, knowing, shivering from the thick blackness that still surrounded us.

"Don't let go."

"Never," he swore, his mouth pressed to my ear. "I'm here; I will always be here, my love." I pressed closer, comforted by his truth. Jackson held me close as he began to walk me out of the room. We stayed like that, desperately locked together, the entire walk out.

I finally opened my eyes and gasped in horror as I saw Caiden struggling towards us unsteadily, madness in his gaze. He was holding the gun.

"Jackson," I gasped.

Jackson let me go and whirled around, a look of horror on his face as he stared at his brother. "Put the gun down, Caiden. You aren't going to kill me."

"I'll do anything for her to be mine," Caiden responded roughly. Jackson had hit him hard with the bat he'd brought, and it was obvious with the way he was limping that he'd been really injured.

"Caiden, please," I whispered desperately.

He turned his focus on me. "Why can't you look at me like that...touch me like that? Why can't you love me like that?"

"I'm so sorry," I responded, meaning it with everything in me.

Jackson chose that moment to lunge at Caiden while he was distracted, knocking him to the ground and grabbing Caiden's wrist until he dropped the gun. They both scrambled for it, and I stood there watching the carnage in horror, not knowing what to do.

Jackson finally stood up, victorious, the gun in his hand, blood dripping from a cut on his cheek. He pointed the gun at Caiden, determination in his gaze.

I froze for a moment, the scene laid out before me like a tableau created by my worst nightmare.

No. Jackson can't do this.

"Jackson, drop the gun," I begged, my heart beating out of my chest as Jackson stood over his brother's body, the gun trembling in his hand. "You can't do it. You can't kill him."

"He deserves it," Jackson said lifelessly.

"Perhaps, but you can't be the one to make that decision. Please, just drop the gun and come here."

It seemed like a lifetime passed, but Jackson finally dropped the gun and stumbled away from Caiden, falling to the ground in front of me and burying his head in my stomach as great, racking sobs erupted from his body from the horror of what had almost just happened.

I shivered, relief flooding my veins. It wasn't just Caiden that would have been gone if Jackson had fired that gun, it was Jackson too. He never would have recovered from killing his brother.

Caiden lifted his head up with a groan, and his gaze met mine.

I froze because the gun was right by Caiden.

Caiden stared at me, and so many emotions flickered across his face that it was impossible to trace them.

I didn't see it coming, couldn't have seen it coming. By the time I recognized the resignation and abject sorrow in his gaze, it was too late.

Caiden picked up that gun, keeping his gaze on me the entire time. "I love you, Everly James. I'll love you forever and ever. And maybe one day, you'll meet me in the beyond, and you'll finally love me too," he whispered.

"Caiden, *no!*" I screamed, realizing what he was going to do.

But it was too late.

A single shot rang through the air as Caiden Parker put a bullet in his brain.

Only News. Never Opinions.   **05 April**

Dayton Valley News

Your Best Source of News Since 1965

Former South High Football Star Dead at 20 After Miracle Recovery.

Former South High Star, Caiden Parker is dead at twenty. His family has not released his cause of death. A representative for the family asked for privacy at this time. Parker's funeral will be held on Friday at 2:00pm at Dayton Memorial Cemetary.

Parker was a South High Football Star before a car wreck put him in a coma for two years. Parker had made a miraculous recovery just a few months before his tragic death. He was attending Rutherford Academy and planned on playing for the football team in the 2021 season with his twin brother, Rutherford All-Star, Jackson Parker. "We at Rutherford Academy will -
Story Cont. G7

23

It was raining when we buried him. The mud from the freshly dug grave sloshed on my black flats as I stood in front of his headstone. I attended the funeral by myself, in the back of the crowd, hidden from view under an umbrella.

Jackson had gone black the day his twin died, and he still wasn't back.

I watched the funeral attendees gather around, all of them mourning the boy they thought they knew instead of the man he actually was.

"How terrible."

"Such a loss."

"He was so young."

They whispered their comments, all ignoring the fact that Caiden had been a kidnapper. An attempted murderer...that he killed himself. They created their own stories for who he'd been, trying to give themselves relief, to make sense of the tragedy of it all.

Jackson's parents stood by the grave, wrapped in their grief, his mother's tears never-ending.

It was terrible.

I hovered in the back, knowing that my presence would be most unwelcome. I let all of these strangers have their moment, and I waited patiently for mine.

And finally, when all of the attendees had left to go to whatever lavish wake was waiting for them, I approached his grave.

I kneeled in front of it, the cold mud seeping into my thin black tights. I traced the letters on the stone with my hand, wanting to cry but unable to summon any more tears.

"I hope you're able to forget me up there, that you find the peace I couldn't give you," I whispered to him. "I'm so fucking sorry I couldn't be what you wanted."

The tears I thought I'd cried out finally came then as I wept for the boy I once knew and the monster he'd become.

I had so much anger, so much disgust, but I let it go as I knelt in front of his grave.

The rain finally stopped at some point, and sunlight peeked through the previously thick, dark clouds.

And it felt like a sign.

I turned my face towards the sunlight, and I sent up my love to Caiden, hoping that wherever he was, he would feel it.

It wasn't the love that he'd wanted, but it was all I had to give.

"Goodbye, Caiden," I whispered to the heavens.

And then I picked myself up from the sodden ground, dropping Caiden's diamond ring to the ground in front of his grave, leaving it behind with all my guilt and my fears, knowing they had no place in my future.

Jackson was waiting for me.

It was days before I saw blue in Jackson's gaze. We were lying in his bed, my body wrapped around his, my soul asking him desperately to return to me.

And when he finally did, it was a beautiful thing.

He took my hand and brushed a kiss across my skin, and we wept together. He stretched towards me for a kiss, soft at first, and then deeper, his tongue sweeping against mine lazily, like we could do this every day, like we had forever in front of us.

And for the first time, I knew we did.

I didn't know where we went from here, but I knew wherever it was, it would be together.

Because when we were together, no matter where together was, it was home.

Our journey to a happily ever after was not the stuff of fairy tales, but it was ours. And it was enough.

It was more than enough.

Our love wasn't the stuff of fairy tales.

It was the stuff of legends.

EPILOGUE

I married him amongst the wildflowers in that field where we'd found our way back to each other.

It was just him and me, and the preacher, just like we'd talked about that day.

And I did run to him, as fast as I could, to where he was standing there with the blue sky behind him, the breeze blowing in his golden hair, a lifetime of happily ever after just a few words away.

Jackson was twenty and I was nineteen, and people said we were too young.

But we knew better.

We'd lived what had felt like a thousand years already, so there was no need to wait a second longer than necessary to start our new life together.

And what a beautiful life it turned out to be.

"You can now recite your vows, Jackson," Reverend Calhoon said with a smile.

Jackson blinked, tears gathering in his eyes as he gazed down at me, more love than I could ever comprehend in their depths.

"I promise to never forget that you are my dream, the best

thing that has ever happened to me, and will ever happen to me. I promise to always put you first, to remind you every day that you are loved. I promise to listen to you, to be there for you, to love you far beyond my last breath. I promise you, Everly James, that I will always do my best to make all the rest of your days happy ones. I love you, Everly. Always."

A soft sob was in his words, and I promised myself I would remember his vows and keep them close to me...always.

"Everly," the reverend prodded with a soft smile after I continued to stand there, just staring at Jackson and wondering how it was possible to feel this much love for one person.

I cleared my throat, knowing that no matter what I did, my words were going to be threaded with tears.

"Jackson. My heartbreak prince," I started, eliciting a small laugh from Jackson's beautiful mouth. "I vow to stand by you no matter where life takes us. To find you in the darkness and always bring you home. I promise to be true to you and never forget that our love is one that I've fought almost my whole life to get to keep. You are my beginning and my end. My daylight in a life once filled with only night. I'll love you, Jackson Parker. Always."

Jackson went pro his junior year at Rutherford, and I followed him to New York City, where he was the starting quarterback for the New York Giants his rookie year. They allowed me to take my classes online, since Jackson was such a big deal. I changed my major to English Literature, realizing that the last thing I wanted was to spend the next ten years in school.

I wanted to write.

And write I did.

The first book I published was our love story.

Jackson, my golden prince, did his best to fill all my days with happiness, just like he'd promised.

But sometimes, despite our best efforts to forget, something would remind us of Caiden and we would both cry over the beautiful brown-eyed boy that we couldn't save.

And sometimes, in dreams, I would meet Caiden in sweet conversations, reminiscent of our childhood and the boy I'd thought I knew...and it wouldn't hurt.

The years took their sweet time erasing the memory of Caiden.

And maybe that was okay.

Maybe we were supposed to remember the good, the bad, and everything in between.

Just so we never forgot to treasure what we had right now.

Days filled with so much joy and love that they seemed like a dream.

And as Jackson stroked my rounded stomach, whispering to the little girl we'd be having in two short months, I smiled, wondering how the girl from the wrong side of the tracks had ended up with the prince after all.

Like I said, it was a beautiful life.

The End.

Only News. Never Opinions.   08 July

Dayton Valley News

Your Best Source of News Since 1965

Local Football Star Turned College Phenom Marries High School Sweetheart

Former South High Star turned College Superstar, Jackson Parker, announced his marriage to high school sweetheart Everly James. Parker, 20, and James, 19, married in an undisclosed location a week ago. Jackson has recently been drafted to the New York Giants and will start training camp after the couple gets back from their two-week honeymoon in St. Lucia. Parker and James had been attending Rutherford Academy together prior to the engagement. Parker recently lost his twin brother to a tragic accident after his miraculous recovery from a two-year coma. Source- Story Cont. A 4

Only News. Never Opinions. **03 March**

Dayton Valley News
Your Best Source of News Since 1965

Former South High Student Makes New York Times Bestseller's List

Former Dayton resident, Everly James, has made waves in the literary world with the debut release of her novel, Heartbreak Prince. James, who attended South High and the prestigious Rutherford Academy made the New York Times Bestseller's List after selling twenty-thousand copies in her first week on the market. Heartbreak Prince, a novel that James has said in past interviews is based on her own love story with NFL football star Jackson Parker, tell the story of an abused girl torn between a set of twin brothers. James's husband lost his twin brother to suicide just-
Story Cont. A2

CAIDEN POV-EXTRA SCENE

Join my newsletter to get a scene from Caiden's POV.

Sign up here.

.

C.R. JANE'S ACKNOWLEDGEMENTS

Sad, Beautiful, Tragic.

I hope the imagery of this book was as clear in your head as it was in mine. I didn't start off knowing that Caiden would die. But then I was listening to Sad, Beautiful, Tragic...by Taylor Swift of course, and I saw it. I saw Everly kneeling by that grave. I saw the rain falling down. I saw Jackson and Everly mourning the boy they couldn't save.

It gutted me.

I agonized and tossed and turned at night debating what to do.

And eventually I just knew this was the only way this book could end.

I love to write those moments that hurt the soul because they're so beautiful and terrible at the same time.

This duet will haunt me for a long time.

I hope I made you feel...and that you don't hate me too much.

A huge thank you to Summer E. for beta reading the hell out of this book. I had fun ending excerpts on the worst possible cliff hanger so she was constantly screaming at me. Summer, thank you for your insight, encouragement, and love for my book baby. You are incredible.

Another thank you to Caitlin, the best P.A. and friend a girl could ask for. You're loyal, hard-working, and you let me vent. You're basically perfect.

Thank you to Heather and Megan as usual. You meet my crazy deadlines and always support me. You make my books sparkle and shine and be the best they can be.

And as always...thank you to my Fates (my readers). You support me, you love me even when I do cliffhangers, and I wouldn't be here if it weren't for you. Love you guys.

Keep Reading for a Look at Remember Us This Way, Book 1 of the completed Sound of Us Series

The Sound of Us Book 1

REMEMBER US THIS WAY

International Bestselling Author
C.R. Jane

Remember Us This Way by C. R. Jane

Copyright © 2019 by C. R. Jane

All rights reserved.

No portion of this book may be reproduced in any form or by any electronic or mechanical means, including information storage and retrieval systems, without written permission from the author, except for the use of brief quotations in a book review, and except as permitted by U.S. copyright law.

For permissions contact:

crjaneauthor@gmail.com

This book is a work of fiction. Names, characters, businesses, places, events, locales, and incidents are either the products of the author's imagination or used in a fictitious manner. Any resemblance to actual persons, living or dead, or actual events is purely coincidental.

REMEMBER US THIS WAY

They are idols to millions worldwide. I hear their names whispered in the hallways and blasted through the radio. Their faces are never far from the television screen, tormenting me with images of what I gave up.

To everyone else, they're unattainable rockstars, the music gods who make up The Sound of Us. But to me? They'll always be the boys I lost.

I broke all our hearts when I refused to follow them to L.A., convinced I would only bring them down. Years later, after I've succumbed to a monster, and my life has become something out of a nightmare, they are back.

I'm no longer the girl they left behind. But what if I've become the woman they can't forget?

PROLOGUE

According to the Sounds of Us Wikipedia page, the band hit almost instant stardom as soon as they finished recording their first album. A small indie band that had gained only regional notoriety, Red Label had taken a huge risk by signing them. The good looks and the killer voices of the three band members combined with the chance at a larger platform ended up making Sounds of Us the Label's most successful band in history. They released their first album, Death by Heartbreak, in 2013, and the first single, Follow You Into the Dark, made it to the Billboard Top 100 immediately.

It was their second single that propelled Sounds of Us to legend status though. Cold Heart was number one on the charts almost the second it was released. That led to four other songs ending up in the top ten. Three of them reached number one, with a fourth hitting number two on the charts. That album was torture in its finest form for me. Partly because I had lost them, but also partly because every one of those songs was about me. And that was just the hits. There were a lot more references in the songs that never got released as singles. It was a sharp stab in the chest to hear songs blaring from radios – songs whose lyrics contained exact words each of them had said to me, and that I had said to them.

And while some of the songs were wistful and pained, others were angry. Pissed-off. Occasionally enraged. It was uncomfortable. Actually, it was excruciating. At least for the first couple of months. I stopped listening to music eventually, something that had meant the world to me my entire life. I just couldn't handle the reminder of them anymore. My heart couldn't take it.

But every so often, a car would go by with its window down, or I'd walk past a motel room playing the radio, and I'd hear one of their voices and it would be an unexpected jolt of pain all over again.

After the release of their album, the band embarked on a short European tour, then followed it up with a much larger American tour. They started selling out stadiums. They appeared on every late-night show there was. Everyone wanted a piece of them. They were like this generation's Beatles, probably even bigger. The next two albums certainly were bigger, although those were easier for me to listen to since the songs about me faded as time went on. They were the most celebrated band in the world and there was no sign of their success slowing down anytime soon. It was everything they had ever dreamed about and that I had dreamed about with them.

They lived up to the bad boy image their label wanted to sell. Rumors of drug use and rampant women kept the gossip sites busy. I tried to ignore the magazines in the store racks by the checkout stand, but some of the pictures of the guys stumbling out of clubs with five girls each were a little too damning to be completely unfounded. And of course, there were the rumors that Tanner had secretly been in and out of rehab for the last two years in between tours. Tanner had always struggled with addiction but had only dabbled in hard drugs when I knew him. It wasn't hard for me to picture him struggling with them now that he probably had easy access to whatever he wanted from people desperate to please them all.

I often wondered if any part of the boys I knew were still around after I let myself give into my own addiction of catching up on any Sounds of Us news I could find. And then I would hear about them buying a house for someone who had lost everything in a natural disaster or hear of them participating in a charity drive to keep a no-kill shelter up and running, and I would know that a part of them was still there.

I've never made peace with letting them go. I never will.

CHAPTER 1

I hear the song come on from the living room. I had forgotten I had read that they were performing for New Year's Eve tonight in New York City before they embarked on their North American tour for the rest of the year. I wanted to avoid the room the music was coming from, but not even my hate for its current occupant could keep my feet from wandering to where the song was playing.

As I took that first step into the living room, and I saw Tanner's face up close, my heart clenched. As usual, he was singing to the audience like he was making love to them. When the camera panned to the audience, girls were literally fainting in the first few rows if he so much as ran his eyes in their direction. He swept a lock of his black hair out of his face, and the girls screamed even louder. Tanner had always had the bad boy look down perfectly. Piercing silver eyes that demanded sex, and full pouty lips you couldn't help but fantasize over, he was every mother's worst nightmare and every girl's naughty dream. I devoured his image like I was a crack addict desperate for one more hit. Usually

I avoided them like the plague, but junkies always gave in eventually. I was not the exception.

"See something you like?" comes a cold, amused voice that never ceases to fill me with dread. I curse my weakness at allowing myself to even come in the room. I know better than this.

"Just coming to see if you need a refill of your beer," I tell him nonchalantly, praying that he'll believe me, but knowing he won't.

My husband is sitting in his favorite armchair. He's a good-looking man according to the world's standards. Even I have to admit that despite the fact that the ugliness that lies inside his heart has long prevented me from finding him appealing in any way. His blonde hair is parted to the side perfectly, not a hair out of place. Sometimes I get the urge to mess it up, just so there can be an outward expression of the chaos that hides beneath his skin.

After I let the guys go, there was nothing left for me in the world. Instead of rising above my circumstances and becoming someone they would have been proud of, I became nothing. Gentry made perfectly clear that anything I was now was because of him.

Echoes of my lost heart beat inside my mind as another song starts to play on the television. It's the song that I know they wrote for me. It's angry and filled with betrayal, the kind of pain you don't come back from. The kind of pain you don't forgive.

Too late I realize that Gentry just asked me something and that my silence will tell him that I'm not paying attention to him. The sharp strike of his palm against my face sends me flying to the ground. I press my hand to my cheek as if I can stop the pain that is coursing through me. I already know this one will bruise. I'll have to wear an extra

Heartbreak Lover

layer of makeup to cover it up when Gentry forces me to meet him at the country club tomorrow. After all, we wouldn't want anyone at the club to know that our lives are anything less than perfect.

The song is still going and somehow the pain I hear in Tanner's voice hurts me more than the pain blossoming across my cheek. Would it not hurt them as much if they knew everything I had told them to sever our connection permanently was a lie? Would they even care at this point that I had done it to set them free, to stop them from being dragged down into the hell I never seemed to be able to escape from? At night, when I lay in bed, listening to the sound of Gentry sleeping peacefully as if the world was perfect and monsters didn't exist, I told myself that it would matter.

"Get up," snaps Gentry, yanking me up from the floor. I'm really off my game tonight by lingering. Nothing makes Gentry madder than when I "wallow" as he calls it. As I stumble out of the room, my head spinning a bit from the force of the hit, a sick part of me thinks it was worth it, just so I could hear the end of their song.

§

Later that night, long after I should have fallen asleep, my mind plays back what little of the performance I saw earlier. I wonder if Jensen still gets severe stage fright before he performs. I wonder if Jesse still keeps his lucky guitar pick in his pocket during performances. I wonder who Tanner gets his good luck kiss from now.

It all hurts too much to contemplate for too long so I grab the Ambien I keep on my bedside table for when I can't sleep, which is often, and I drift off into a dreamland filled with a silver eyed boy who speaks straight to my soul.

The next morning comes too early and I struggle to wake up when Gentry's alarm goes off. Ambien always leaves me groggy and I haven't decided what's better, being exhausted from not sleeping, or taking half the day to wake up all the way.

Throwing a robe on, I blurrily walk to the kitchen to get Gentry's protein shake ready for him to take with him to the gym.

I'm standing in front of the blender when Gentry comes up behind me and puts his arms around me, as if the night before never happened. I'm very still, not wanting to make any sudden movement just in case he takes it the wrong way.

"Meet me at the club for lunch," he asks, running his nose up the side of my neck and eliciting shivers...the wrong kind of shivers. He's using his charming voice, the one that always gets everyone to do what he wants. It stopped working on me a long time ago.

"Of course," I tell him, turning in his arms and giving him a wide, fake smile. What else would my answer be when I know the consequences of going against Gentry's wishes?

"Good," he says with satisfaction, placing a quick, sharp kiss on my lips before stepping away.

I pour the blended protein shake into a cup and hand it to him. "11:45?" I ask. He nods and waves goodbye as he walks out of the house to head to the country club gym where he'll spend the next several hours working out with his friends, flirting with the girls that work out there, and overall acting like the overwhelming douche that he is.

I don't relax until the sound of the car fades into the

distance. After eating a protein shake myself (Gentry doesn't approve of me eating carbs), I start my chores for the day before I have to get ready to meet him at the country club.

My hands are red and raw from washing the dishes twice. Everything was always twice. Twice bought me time and ensured there wouldn't be anything left behind. An errant fleck of food, a spot that hadn't been rinsed – these were things he'd notice.

Hours later, I've vacuumed, swept, done the laundry, and cleaned all the bathrooms. Gentry could easily afford a maid, but he likes me to "keep busy" as he puts it, so I do everything in this house of horrors. I repeat the same things every day even though the house is in perfect condition. I would clean every second if it meant that he was out of the house permanently though.

I straighten the pearls around my neck and think for the thousandth time that if I ever escape this hell hole, I'm going to burn every pearl I come across. I'm dressed in a fitted pastel pink dress that comes complete with a belt ordained with daisies. Five years ago, I wouldn't have been caught dead in such an outfit but far be it for me to wear jeans to a country club. I slip into a pair of matching pastel wedges and then run out to the car. I'm running late and I can only hope that he's distracted and doesn't realize the time.

As I drive, I can't help but daydream. Dream about what it would have been like if I had joined the guys in L.A. Bellmont is a sleepy town that's been the same for generations. I haven't been anywhere outside of the town since I got married except to Myrtle Beach for my honeymoon.

The town is steeped in history, a history that it's very proud of. The main street is still perfectly maintained from the early 1900s, and I've always loved the whitewashed look of the buildings and the wooden shingles on every roof. The town attracts a vast array of tourists who come here to be close to the beach. They can get a taste of the coastal southern flavor of places like Charleston and Charlotte, but they don't have to pay as high of a price tag.

It's a beautiful prison to me, and if I ever manage to escape from it, I never want to see it again.

I turn down a street and start down the long drive that leads to Bellmont's most exclusive country club. The entire length of the road is sheltered by large oak trees and it never ceases to make me feel like an extra in Gone With the Wind whenever I come here. The feeling is only reinforced when I pull up to the large, freshly painted white plantation house that's been converted into the club.

My blood pressure spikes as I near the valet stand. Just knowing that I'm about to see Gentry and all of his friends is enough to send my pulse racing. I smile nervously at the teenage boy who is manning the stand and hand him my keys. He gives me a big smile and a wink. It reminds me of something that Jesse used to do to older women to make them swoon, and my heart clenches. Is there ever going to be a day when something doesn't remind me of one of them?

I ignore the valet boy's smile and walk inside, heading to the bar where I can usually find Gentry around lunch time. I pause as I walk inside the lounge. Wendy Perkinson is leaning against Gentry, pressing her breasts against him, much too close for propriety's sake. I know I should probably care at least a little bit, but the idea of Gentry turning his attentions away from me and on to Wendy permanently is more than I can even wish for. I'm sure he's fucked her, the way she's practically salivating over him as he talks to his friend blares it loudly, but unfortunately that's all she will

Heartbreak Lover

ever get from him. Gentry's obsession with me has thus far proved to be a lasting thing. But since I finally started refusing to sleep with him after the beatings became a regular thing, he goes elsewhere for his so-called needs when he doesn't feel like trying to force me. At least a few times a week I'm assaulted by the stench of another woman's perfume on my husband's clothes. It's become just another unspoken thing in my marriage.

Martin, Gentry's best friend, is the first to see me and his eyes widen when he does. He coughs nervously, the poor thing thinking I actually care about the situation I've walked into. Gentry looks at him and then looks at the entrance where he sees me standing there. His eyes don't widen in anything remotely resembling remorse or shame...we're too far past that at this point. He does extricate himself from Wendy's grip however to start walking towards me, his gaze devouring me as he does so. One thing I've never doubted in my relationship with Gentry is how beautiful he thinks I am.

"You're gorgeous," he tells me, kissing me on the cheek and putting a little too much pressure on my arm as he guides me to the bar. Wendy has moved farther down the bar, setting her sights on another married member of the club. It's funny to me that in high school I had wanted to stab her viciously when she set her sights on Jesse, but when she actually sleeps with my husband I could care less.

"My parents are waiting in the dining hall. You're ten minutes late," says Gentry, again squeezing my arm to emphasize his displeasure with me. I sigh, pasting the fake smile on my face that I know he expects. "There was traffic," I say simply, and I let him lead me to the dining hall where the second worst thing about Gentry is waiting for us.

Gentry's mother, Lucinda, considers herself southern

royalty. Her parents owned the largest plantation in South Carolina and spoiled their only daughter with everything that her heart desired. This of course made her perhaps the most self-obsessed woman I had ever met, and that was putting it lightly. Gentry's father, Conrad, stands as we approach, dressed up in the suit and tie that he wears everywhere regardless of the occasion. Like his son, Gentry's father was a handsome man. Although his hair was slightly greying at the temples, his face remained impressively unlined, perhaps due to the same miracle worker that made his wife look forever thirty-five.

"Darling, you look wonderful as always," he tells me, brushing a kiss against my cheek and making we want to douse myself in boiling water. Conrad had no qualms about propositioning his son's wife. I couldn't remember an interaction I'd had with him that hadn't ended with him asking me to sneak away to the nearest dark corner with him. I purposely choose to sit on the other side of Gentry, next to his mother, although that option isn't much better. She looks me over, pursing her lips when she gets to my hair. According to her, a proper southern lady keeps her hair pulled back. But I've never been a proper lady, and the guys always loved my hair. Keeping it down is my silent tribute to them and the person I used to be since everything else about me is almost unrecognizable.

Lucinda is a beautiful woman. She's always impeccably dressed, and her mahogany hair is always impeccably coiffed. She's also as shallow as a teacup. She begins to chatter, telling me all about the town gossip; who's sleeping with who, who just got fake boobs, whose husband just filed for bankruptcy. It all passes in one ear and out the other until I hear her say something that sounds unmistakably like "Sounds of Us."

I look up at her, catching her off guard with my sudden interest. "Sorry, could you repeat that?" I ask. Her eyes are gleaming with excitement as she clasps her hands delicately in front of herself. She waits to speak until the waiter has refilled her glass with water. She slowly takes a sip, drawing out the wait now that she actually has my attention.

"I was talking about the Sounds of Us concert next week. They are performing two shows. Everyone's going crazy over the fact that the boys will be coming home for the first time since they made it big. It's been what...four years?" she says.

"Five," I correct her automatically, before cursing myself when she smirks at me.

"So, you aren't immune to the boys' charms either..." she says with a grin.

"What was that, Mother?" asks Gentry, his interest of course rising at the mention of anything to do with me and other men.

"I was just telling Ariana about the concert coming to town," she says. I hold my breath waiting to hear if she will mention the name. Gentry's so clueless about anything that doesn't involve him that he probably hasn't heard yet that they're coming to town.

"Ariana doesn't like concerts," he says automatically. It's his go-to excuse for making sure I never attend any social functions that don't involve him. Ariana doesn't like sushi. Ariana doesn't like movies. The list of times he's said such a thing go on and on. I feel a slight pang in my chest. Ariana. Gentry and his family insist on calling me by my full name, and I miss the days where I had relationships that were free and easy enough to use my nickname of Ari.

"Of course she doesn't, dear," says Lucinda, patting my hand. The state of my marriage provides much amusement to Lucinda and Conrad. Both approve of the Gentry's "heavy hand" towards me and although they haven't witnessed the abuse first hand, they're well aware of Gentry's penchant for using me as a punching bag. Gentry's parents are simply charming.

I pick at my salad and listen to Lucinda prattle on, my interest gone now that she's off the subject of the concert. Gentry and his dad are whispering back and forth, and I can feel Gentry shooting furtive glances at me. I know I should be concerned or at least interested about what their talking about, but my mind has taken off, thinking about the fact that in just a few days' time, the guys will be in the same vicinity as me for the first time in five years. If only....

"Ariana," says Gentry, pulling me from my day dream. I immediately pull on the smile I have programmed to flash whenever I'm in public with Gentry.

"Yes?"

"I think you've had enough to eat," he tells me as if he's talking about the weather and not the fact that he's just embarrassed me in front of everyone at the table.

I shakily set my fork down, my cheeks flushing from his comment. I was eating a salad and I'm already slimmer than I should be. But Gentry loves to control everything about me, food being just one of many things. I see Lucinda patting her lips delicately as she finishes eating her salmon. My stomach growls at the fact that I've had just a few bites to eat. I have a few dollars stashed away in my car, I'll have to stop somewhere and grab something to eat on the way home. That is if Gentry doesn't leave at the same time as me and follow me.

When I've gotten my emotions under control, I finally lift my eyes and glance at my husband. He's back in deep conversation with Conrad, their voices still too soft for me to pick anything up. Looking at him, I can't help but get the urge to stab him with my silverware and then run screaming from the room. The bastard would probably find a way to haunt me from the grave even if he didn't survive. Still, I find my hand clenching involuntarily as if grasping for a phantom knife.

After that one terrible night when it became clear that I couldn't go to L.A. to meet up with the guys, I was lost. I got a job as a waitress and was living in one of those pay by week extended stay motels since there was no way I could stay in my trailer with *them* anymore. I met Gentry Mayfield while waitressing one night. He was handsome and charming, and persevered in asking me out even when I refused the first half a dozen times. My heart was broken, how could I even think of trying to give my broken self to someone else? I finally got tired of saying no and went on a date with him. He made me smile, something that I didn't think was possible, and every date after that seemed to be more perfect than I deserved. I didn't fall in love with Gentry, my heart belonged to three other men, but I did develop admiration and fondness for Gentry in a way that I hadn't thought possible. After pictures started to surface on the first page of the gossip sites of the guys with hordes of beautiful women, and the fact that my life seemed to be going nowhere, marrying Gentry seemed to be the second chance that I didn't deserve. Except the funny thing about how it all turned out is that my life with Gentry turned out worse than I probably deserved, even after everything that had happened.

Three months after we were married, I burnt dinner. Gentry had come home in a bad mood because of something that had happened at work. Apparently, me burning dinner was the last straw for him that day and he struck me across the face, sending me flying to the ground. Afterwards, he begged and pleaded with me for forgiveness, saying it would never happen again. But I wasn't stupid, I knew how this story played out. I stayed for a week so that I could get ahold of as much money as I could and then I drove off while he was at work. I was stopped at the state lines by a trooper who evidently was friends with Gentry's family. I was dragged kicking and screaming back home where Gentry was waiting, furious and ready to make me pay. Every semblance of the man that I had thought I was marrying was gone.

I had $5,000 to my name when I met him. I'd gotten it from selling the trailer that I inherited when my parents died in a car crash after one of their drunken nights out on the town. Gentry had convinced me that I should put it in our "joint account" right after we got married and stupidly, I had agreed to do it. I never got access to that account. Gentry stole my money, he stole my self-esteem. No, he didn't steal it, he chipped away at it and just when I thought I'd crumble, he kissed me and cried over me and told me he'd die without me.

I tried to get away several more times, by bus, on foot, I even went to the police to try and report him. But the Mayfield's had everyone in this state in their pocket, and nothing I said or did worked. I eventually stopped trying. It had taken me a year of not running away to get my car back and to be able to do things other than stay home, locked in our bedroom, while Gentry was at work.

Gentry stood up from the table, bringing me back to the present. A random song lyric floated through my mind about how the devil wears a pretty face, it certainly fit Gentry Mayfield.

"I'm heading to the office for the rest of the day. What

are your plans?" he asks, as if I had a choice in what my plans were.

"Just finishing things around the house and going to the store to get a few ingredients for dinner," I tell him, waving a falsely cheerful goodbye to Gentry's parents as he walks me out of the dining area towards the valet stand. We stop by the exit and he pulls me towards him, stroking the side of my face that I've painted with makeup to hide the bruise he gave me the night before. My eyes flutter from the rush of pain but Gentry somehow mistakes it as the good kind of reaction to his touch. He leans in for a kiss.

"You're still the most beautiful woman I've ever seen," he tells me, sealing his lips over mine in a way that both cuts off my air supply and makes me want to wretch all at once. I hold still, knowing that it will enrage him that I don't do anything in response to his kiss, but not having it in me to fake more than I already have for the day. He pulls back and searches my eyes for something, I'm not sure what. He must not find it because his own eyes darken, and his grip on my arms suddenly tightens to a point that wouldn't look like anything to a club passerby, but that will inevitably leave bruises on my too pale skin.

He leans in and brushes his lips against my ear. "You're never going to get away from me, so when are you going to just give in?" he spits out harshly. I say nothing, just stare at him stonily. I can see the storm building in his eyes.

"Don't bother with dinner, I'll be home late," he says, striding away without a second glance, probably to go find Wendy and make plans to fuck her after he leaves the office, or maybe it will be at the office knowing him.

I wearily make my way through the doors to the valet stand and patiently wait for my keys. It's a different kid this time and I'm grateful he doesn't try to flirt with me.

On my way back from the country club I find myself taking the long way back to the house, the way that takes me by the trailer park where I grew up. I park by the office trailer and find myself walking to the field behind the rows of homes. Looking at the trash riddled ground, I gingerly walk through the mud, flecks of it hitting the formerly pristine white fabric of my shoes. I walk until I get to an abandoned fire pit that doesn't look like it's been used for quite a while. For probably five years to be exact.

I sit on a turned over trash barrel until the sun sits precariously low in the sky and I know that I'm playing with fire if I dare to stay any longer. I then get up and walk back to my car, passing by the trailer I once lived in. It's funny that after everything that has happened, at the moment I would give anything to be back in that trailer again.

Discover the rest of this **COMPLETED** series at
books2read.com/rememberusthisway

ABOUT C.R. JANE

A Texas girl living in Utah now, I'm a wife, mother, lawyer, and now author. My stories have been floating around in my head for years, and it has been a relief to finally get them down on paper. I'm a huge Dallas Cowboys fan and I primarily listen to Beyonce and Taylor Swift...don't lie and say you don't too.

My love of reading started probably when I was three and with a faster than normal ability to read, I've devoured hundreds of thousands of books in my life. It only made sense that I would start to create my own worlds since I was always getting lost in others'. I like heroines who have to grow in order to become badasses, happy endings, and swoon-worthy, devoted, (and hot) male characters. If this sounds like you, I'm pretty sure we'll be friends. I'm so glad to have you on my team...check out the links below for ways to hang out with me and more of my books you can read!

Visit my **Facebook** page to get updates.
    Visit my **Amazon Author** page.
    Visit my **Website**.
    Sign up for my **newsletter** to stay updated on new releases, find out random facts about me, and get access to different points of view from my characters.

OTHER BOOKS BY C.R. JANE

The Fated Wings Series

First Impressions

Forgotten Specters

The Fallen One (a Fated Wings Novella)

Forbidden Queens

Frightful Beginnings (a Fated Wings Short Story)

Faded Realms

Faithless Dreams

Fabled Kingdoms

The Rock God (a Fated Wings Novella)

The Timeless Affection Series

Lamented Pasts

Lost Passions

The Sounds of Us Contemporary Series (complete series)

Remember Us This Way

Remember You This Way

Remember Me This Way

Broken Hearts Academy Series

Heartbreak Prince

Heartbreak Lover

Ugly Hearts Series: Enemies to Lovers

Ugly Hearts

The Pack Queen Series

Queen of the Thieves (2020)

Academy of Souls Co-write with Mila Young (complete series)

School of Broken Souls

School of Broken Hearts

School of Broken Dreams

School of Broken Wings

Fallen World Series Co-write with Mila Young (complete series)

Bound

Broken

Betrayed

Belong

Thief of Hearts Co-write with Mila Young

Siren Condemned

Siren Sacrificed

Siren Awakened

Stupid Boys Series Co-write with Rebecca Royce

Stupid Boys

Dumb Girl

Crazy Love

Breathe Me Duet Co-write with Ivy Fox (complete)

Breathe Me

Breathe You

Printed in Dunstable, United Kingdom